# Ancient Warlord

Ancients Rising Series, #10

## Katie Reus

# DEDICATION

*This one is for the Vancleave Library – thank you for supporting authors (and me, specifically). Librarians really are magic.*

# CHAPTER 1

*Dear Princess...*

No, Mia scratched the words out, then set the fine paper aside. She didn't want to waste it, but her friend had told her to stop calling her princess. It was very hard, however, especially since she was currently in the opulent sitting room in the Nova Castle that Stella's family owned.

Or *one* of the castles. But this was the main one and gorgeous didn't even begin to cover it. There were stained-glass windows everywhere depicting dragons in various states of battle. Sometimes they were simply flying, but for the most part the scenes were full of carnage.

Years ago, when supernaturals had come out to the world in what became known as The Fall, Mia hadn't been surprised. She was from New Orleans after all, and had known about some of the things that went bump in the night already.

Not dragons though.

That had been a whole new discovery.

Then new non-human realms had opened themselves up to certain human territories, including the Nova realm, run by a fierce matriarchal line of dragons.

And Mia had been lucky enough to be invited to live here as long as she wanted because of her artistic talent. She couldn't see herself ever wanting to leave, even if this place was ridiculously cold. Even their spring and summers were chilly.

Which was why she was sitting near a roaring fireplace that was three times her size at least, curled up with hot tea as she waited for Starlena, who had asked her to meet at the castle.

Since she had time to kill, she'd decided to write a letter to Stella in the meantime, the reason Mia was here at all.

*Dear Stella,*

*I received your last letter and couldn't help but laugh at Christian's antics. I'm so happy that you and Rhodes are settling in and that you're keeping Christian company. He shouldn't be in that big house by himself anyway. It sounds as if the city has welcomed you with open arms. And I must confess I miss New Orleans every time I read one of your letters.*

*But not enough to return just yet (maybe ever). There's so much to explore in your realm and I feel as if it will take a hundred years to even scrape the surface. The artists' enclave has welcomed me to the point where they all feel like family. And I know you were worried about the way dragons would react to having humans in the realm, but no one has made me feel othered because I'm human.*

Mia paused in her writing, her face growing hot. Then she continued.

*Well, no one except a giant jerk named Tiber. I know I shouldn't care, but I guess after having known so many supernaturals who have been so welcoming, it just jarred me to hear him saying horrible things about humans. One bad apple out of the hundreds of dragons I've come in contact with isn't terrible, so I hope that sets your mind at ease.*

Mia wondered if she should have mentioned the annoyingly good-looking Tiber at all, but whatever, she needed to vent. And she and Stella had developed a genuine relationship where they filled each other in on the comings and goings of their respective territories. She loved hearing about everyone back home and Stella had told her she enjoyed the same.

So Mia filled her in with the little tidbits she'd heard around the castle, including new matings, new births, and what Starlena, Soleil and Juniper were up to. Stella's grandmother, mother and sister, respectively. Three royal dragons who were terrifying but also wonderful.

Once she was done, she sealed her letter and set it in her bag. At first it had been a novelty to send handwritten letters, but she could admit that she loved it now.

Just as she stretched her legs out, Valentina, the right-hand woman to Queen Soleil strode in wearing a long, dark-blue tunic and matching pants. Along both hems were intricate silvery embroidery that shimmered against the firelight and sunlight streaming in from some of the high windows. Her long dark hair was pulled up in a complicated coil on top of her head and she had two blades strapped to her thighs. She might be a badass warrior, but her smile was warm.

"Mia, I hope you didn't mind the wait."

"Not at all," she said as she stood, smothering a yawn. "I took the time to write a letter."

"I can post it for you if you'd like."

"Oh, no, I couldn't bother you." Mia knew how busy Valentina was. Mailing letters couldn't possibly be on her list of things to do.

The other woman simply held out her hand. "You are one of the few people in this castle who isn't a bother to me. I would be happy to."

She laughed lightly and reached into her bag. "Well, okay then. I can't say no to that."

"Are you excited about the auction?" Valentina asked as they headed down the long stone corridor lined with gorgeous art and more stained-glass windows.

"Ah, yes." Mostly. She got a little overwhelmed in large crowds and this coming week, starting tonight, was five full days of art festivities, including an auction of sorts. Which would feature her newest paintings. Putting her work on display for a bunch of strangers was terrifying.

"Don't be nervous. Queen Soleil allowed some of your work to be shown early and most of the castle patrons are foaming at the mouth to buy all the paintings they've seen so far. If they have their way you'll never leave our realm," she said on a laugh.

Mia laughed with her but couldn't squash the tension in her stomach. She really, really hated crowds and making small talk. She just wanted to paint, to create.

Not talk to a bunch of strangers. No matter how nice they were. She was good one on one, enjoyed it even. It was just that when there were more than ten people, the noise tended to make it hard for her to focus on what people were saying.

But that was the price of being allowed to live here. Or that was what she told herself. She thought that if she let Starlena know how she felt she could probably miss some of the "festivities" but she didn't want to rock the boat. Not when things were going so well and she was staying here as a guest.

Valentina finally stopped in front of a doorway and knocked once before pushing it open. "Starlena will show you the way out once you're done." She patted Mia's arm gently before heading back down the corridor and disappearing from sight.

"Come in, come in. And she's right. I'll make sure you don't get lost this time."

Mia found herself flushing in embarrassment even though it was true. And she knew it was the reason Valentina had escorted her to Starlena's office—because she'd gotten lost the last *three* times. "This place is a maze," she murmured.

"True enough." Starlena was tall in the way most dragons were, with grayish-silver hair, pale blue eyes that occasionally flashed silver, and possessed a deep magic that even Mia could feel.

Mia had heard rumors about the female, that she possessed a power that could control some supernaturals, force them to speak the truth, that her magic could pull beings back from Hell portals. Considering Mia had seen the dragon release magical glowing chains from her wrists while in human form, she believed everything she'd heard about the ancient female.

"Is everything okay for tonight?" she asked, unable to stop the nerves spreading through her. And why wouldn't she be nervous? Starlena was the mother of the queen, had been leader herself centuries ago, and now governed an elite guard of assassins who lived in the shadows. As far as Mia knew, she'd never met any of them.

Except Tiber, and he didn't count. Because he sucked.

"Oh yes, of course. I've never seen some of our patrons so excited." She motioned to a plush-looking sofa that was large enough to hold three dragons in human form. "Sit, sit," she said as she bustled around the militantly neat office, opening the doors to a large armoire.

Smiling, Starlena pulled out a long, elegant green gown with glittering embroidery along the deep V between the breasts and along the hem. She held it up and looked at Mia expectantly. "What do you think?"

Mia was surprised the warrior was asking her at all. She figured the woman had people for this, but she nodded. "It's a beautiful dress. Stunning. You'll definitely slay in it." To be fair, Mia was pretty sure the woman would kill in anything she wore.

Starlena blinked. "It's for you."

Now Mia was the one to blink and once again she felt her cheeks flushing. She hated feeling like a charity case. Though her brain absolutely knew that this wasn't what this gift was about. But it brought up old insecurities. "It's lovely, beyond so, but I have a dress." One of her artist friends had created an equally stunning gown for her.

"I know, but Soleil has decided that since you are representing the crown, you should match." She motioned to the embroidery of silvery dragons. "We have invited some outsiders to this week's festivities and none of them are human. It's simply a sort of... precaution to let everyone know that you are considered one of us."

"Oh... is there a threat?"

"Not at all, but my daughter and granddaughter adore you. As do I. It's just a precaution, that's all." She shrugged. "We look out for our own."

Warmth spread throughout her middle as she grinned at the ancient woman. "That's the kindest thing you've ever said to me. Thank you for this gift. I will wear it with pride."

Now Starlena looked uncomfortable and cleared her throat. "Yes, well. I won't keep you long—"

They both paused as her door flung open and in stomped Tiber.

And for just a moment, Mia's heart skipped a beat at the sight of him. But come on, she was an artist, she was simply enjoying his form. For purposes of art *only*.

The male was six-five at least and looked as if he'd been carved from marble, though nothing about him was cold. His skin held a light bronze hue and there was just so much of it on display since he was only wearing loose pants and no tunic. Nope, he simply had some sort of leather satchel thing over his incredibly sculpted chest.

And he was staring at her, his amber eyes wide. "Oh, I did not realize you had company." His tone was overly formal and stilted.

And since he was close to Starlena, she would never be anything but ridiculously polite to the male. "It's no interruption." She turned back to Starlena and gave her a real smile. "Thank you again for the gift. I'll just see my way out," she said as she plucked the dress from the outside of the armoire.

And she only cursed a little that she had to go up on tiptoe to grab it. Why was all their furniture so big? Gah.

"If you don't mind, Tiber will show you out?" Starlena said. "I didn't realize he was stopping by and he's going to make himself useful for the interruption."

Tiber simply stared hard at Starlena, but nodded.

Of course, he didn't want to walk her out or be anywhere near her. Mia got it, he hated humans. They were weak and beneath him. Weak and pathetic, he'd once said. "I'm fine, I promise."

"Mia." Starlena lifted an eyebrow.

Okay, so she wasn't fine. She had the world's worst sense of direction. It wasn't just embarrassing, it was a bit debilitating. In fact, it was how she'd overheard a hurtful conversation between Tiber and one of his friends. Months ago, she'd been lost and had ended up in some random training center instead of the art studio she'd been looking for and had overheard his hurtful words.

He already knew how terrible she was with directions. It was probably one of the things he held against her. She was (gasp) human and had no sense of direction. Ugh. Whatever. Screw him.

She pasted on a pleasant smile and turned to the intimidating and far too attractive male. "If you could walk me to the main waiting room, I'll be good from there." Probably. This place really was a labyrinth of corridors and rooms, and everything was just so damn big.

He nodded politely and took the dress from her, holding it up off the ground so the hem wouldn't drag.

"Thank you," she murmured.

And then he proceeded to not say one. Single. Word. For the entire walk out to the courtyard, he didn't utter one.

Though she was grateful he'd walked her to the courtyard because she'd been planning to head in the wrong direction once they passed the room Valentina had picked her up from. Not that she'd ever tell him that.

"Thank you," she said again once they were outside in the waning sunlight.

"Are you good from here?" he growled.

Her cheeks flushed hot from embarrassment—and a little anger. Okay, a lot of anger. Even if it was a fair question. She simply didn't like the way he asked, made her feel less than. He might have a poor view of humans in general, but she'd done nothing to him.

"Yes," she gritted out. Luckily, the walk from the castle to the artists' enclave was a very easy one. She couldn't get lost if she tried.

He grunted again and disappeared back into the castle.

"Good riddance," she muttered, before tucking the gorgeous dress up and under her arms. She had more important things to deal with—like preparing for tonight's party and trying to get her anxiety under control until then.

She wasn't going to waste another thought on the big dragon with amber eyes who despised her.

# CHaPTer 2

Tiber shut the door to Starlena's office, hard.

She grinned at him from her desk, propped her booted feet up on the worn and ancient thing, crossed her ankles.

"I stopped by unexpectedly? You *demanded* I come see you. What the hell?" he said as he moved to one of the serving trays next to the unlit fireplace and grabbed some cheese. She always had the best snacks.

"I was trying to give you an opportunity to speak to Mia. Soooo. What did you two talk about? Did you tell her how lovely she looked today?"

"We didn't talk about anything." He shoved a small block of cheese in his mouth. They had talked about nothing because he couldn't force words out when he was around her. The last time he'd spoken in her presence he'd said unforgiveable things. So now he could not speak at all. Because he was a fool of the worst proportions—and she hated him.

He hated himself a little too.

His oldest friend in the world blinked and set her feet down on the thick rug beneath her desk. "What do you mean, nothing?"

"I... did not say a word."

She blinked again. "Are you telling me that you walked that sweet woman out of here and all the way back to the great hall in complete silence? Just...nothing?"

"I asked her if she needed help once we reached the courtyard and she said she was fine." He swallowed hard. He'd also heard her say "good riddance" to him once he left and his dragon half was currently sulking at her dismissal.

*Not sulking. But you need to do something, to show off for her. She's an artist, I'm sure she wants to paint us. Make yourself useful!*

He ignored his more annoying half. His dragon was wrong and there was nothing he could do to make things right with Mia.

Starlena scrubbed her hands over her face and stood. "I don't know what to do with you!"

"Is that the only reason you called me here? Under false pretenses?" He ate some more cheese. This time he piled the cubes high with meat. He'd finished training his people for the evening, so he didn't mind that he'd been summoned—especially since he'd gotten to see Mia. Still, he had to give Starlena a little shit for it.

"No. It was simply a bonus. I need you to attend the auction tonight. It's much larger than originally planned."

"I'd rather gouge my eyes out with the femur bone of a giant deer."

"That's oddly specific."

"I had my eyes gouged out in a similar fashion before we met." Many years ago, and they'd grown back. "That's how I know I'd prefer it to a party with a bunch of stuffy—"

"Mia will be there."

His dragon perked up. "In that dress I carried for her?"

"Yes."

He frowned. It was a bit showy for the petite human who seemed to prefer to blend in rather than stand out. Though the auburn-haired beauty couldn't blend if she tried. "She won't like it if I'm there." Now that he knew Mia would be there, he was going to go, but he would push back here with Starlena. There was no way he could simply give in to her on this without pushback.

"I need you to be her shadow. The menacing presence that will keep some of the…" She cleared her throat. "More eager patrons at bay. I'm worried that being in a room with so many supernaturals will be overwhelming for her. Our kind aren't the best at giving space."

His dragon bristled with protectiveness at the thought of anything or anyone alarming his petite human. "She lives with dragons and they all have wonderful things to say about her." He knew, because he'd made it his business to know everything about the talented human artist who gave him fake smiles and icy glares. Which he definitely deserved.

"It's not the same and you know it. She lives with artists. They're all…"

He snagged more food. "Soft?"

"I was not going to say that."

Yeah, but she was thinking it.

"Delicate."

Dragons weren't delicate, but he understood her meaning. Dragon shifters weren't a monolith by any means, but some were more savage than others. More deadly. And the artists tended to fall into a different class altogether. Sometimes he thought of them as butterflies, though it was not a completely accurate description. They could turn into dragons after all, could breathe fire, and destroy at will. But more often than not, they lacked the killer instinct as the rest of the species.

"And I'm not concerned about them, but the royals and others who will attend tonight. I'm worried they'll bully her into doing commissions for them."

"It's not like they won't pay her." He tried to keep his tone neutral, as if he didn't care. But if someone tried to bully her, he'd gouge their eyes out and make them eat them. Then once they started to grow back, he'd do it again.

"I know that, but it's not the point. Oh, sweet goddess, why are you arguing with me!" she shouted.

Which was about right. Starlena had patience in spades, except when it came to him. They'd been friends for far too long.

He grinned.

And she threw a paper weight at his head.

Tiber caught it midair. "I'll be there tonight. And you owe me."

"How about if you end up mated to Mia, you'll owe me until your dying breath?" She kicked back in her chair again, looking smug in her power... And he threw the paper weight back at her.

She caught it easily. Her cackling laughter trailed down the hallway as he strode out.

"Stupid fucking auction," he muttered to himself, earning a wide berth from some of the castle staff as he stalked by.

But his dragon half was extremely pleased that he had an excuse to see Mia again.

And the human part didn't exactly hate it either.

***

Tiber resisted the urge to roll his shoulders as he casually walked through the gallery of paintings. The auction tonight was being held in a building directly next to the main castle and it was light and airy—and too full of people at the moment.

The tunic he'd borrowed was snug on his biceps and he regretted wearing a top at all.

If he had his way, he would simply walk around naked all the time. Or at least shirtless. But that was too much, even for dragons. He had to blend at this stuffy affair if he was going to be Mia's shadow.

Unfortunately, he hadn't scented her yet. Or seen her. And it wasn't like he could have called on her, asked to escort her. She would have slammed her door in his face. Or just given him the politest rejection ever. Again, which he deserved.

He really hated himself right now.

"Surprised to see you here." Valentina slid up next to him, wearing a simple silver dress and visible blades on her outer thighs.

In reality, the deadly dragon didn't need them, but they were an outward reminder to everyone that she would and had used them on troublemakers.

"I heard it was going to be quite an auction." He nodded at the picture in front of him, an image painted by Mia that reminded him of his homeland. All rolling dunes of stark desert sand against a backdrop of an inky night sky under a blanket of stars. "And I want this one."

"Ooh, that's a hot ticket. The bidding starts—"

"I don't care. Just make sure I get it." He picked up a drink from a passing waiter holding out a tray. "You know I'm good for it." He was ancient and had been hoarding gold and other shiny things since... he could not even remember how long. He couldn't have Mia, but he would possess her art.

Valentina nodded approvingly. "You have good taste. This human has surprised me. Oh, this is by Mia," she added, pointing to the barely discernible M in the right-hand lower corner.

He simply feigned surprise. No need to let Soleil's spy know that he was obsessed with the beautiful human. "She's quite talented."

"Indeed." Glancing over her shoulder at the growing crowd, she did a quick scan then looked back at him and lowered her voice. "The McIlroy clan is going to offer her a year's commission. The money is obscene, so if you see anything else you like let me know. I have a feeling we won't be seeing anything else of hers for at least a year if she agrees."

Oh, he didn't like that at all. He might not talk to Mia, but he liked watching her. And maybe sometimes he followed her in the shadows while she was out at the market. "Where is she, anyway? I haven't seen her tonight." He hoped his tone came off as bored, when in reality all his muscles were pulled taut at the thought of seeing her, inhaling that sweet, fresh scent that reminded him of orange blossoms. He'd already done one loop around the gallery and hadn't gotten a hint of her scent.

"Oh, she's not here..." Valentina laughed lightly as she turned back to him. "Okay talk about timing. She just walked in. And I see someone I need to talk to. But I've made a note for that painting—it's yours. Fair warning, it's going to cost you."

Tiber turned to find Mia on the arm of Jonothon, a male who created sculptures as beautiful as him.

*Maybe we make a sculpture of his face with our claws,* his dragon snarled.

That doesn't even make sense, he told his other half.

*Fine, how about we rip off his head? Better?*

His dragon was the biggest asshole on the planet. But... his gaze narrowed to where Mia had her fingers gently holding onto Jonothon's forearm. He wouldn't mind bashing the other male's face in. Just a little.

Inevitably, because he had no control where she was concerned, he drank in the sight of her. Every, single, inch.

The bodice of the green dress split right to her midsection in a huge V, revealing the soft swells of her breasts and every step she took, he realized there was a slit in the skirt right up to her left thigh.

He could feel the fire building in him, wondered if Starlena had picked out that... that... *scrap* of material for her to wear in public just to make him crazy. It was obscene and she wore it as if it had been made for her. And goddess, he wanted to shred it and then bring her so much pleasure she never touched or looked at another male.

Because that's how worked up he was, obsessing over a human who hated him.

He ducked out of sight, using his skill as a trained assassin to blend in among the growing throng of assholes. God, when had he turned into such a grumpy dick?

*You've always been like this. Do not pretend otherwise.*

Shut the fuck up, he snarled. He could not deal with that shit tonight when he was trying to keep an eye on Mia.

Her long, auburn hair was piled up on her head in a complicated twist of braids and as he moved in behind her and her date, he realized that the dress dipped even lower in the back, to just above the swell of her hips. Her skin was so smooth, so soft looking and oh, he did not like the other man standing so close to her, his arm wrapped around her delicate shoulders.

At a cracking sound, he looked down and saw that he'd shattered the champagne glass in his hand. He ignored a couple snooty looks and placed the remains on a passing tray. He was supposed to be better at his job than this.

For the next hour he remained in the shadows, watching Mia talk to a handful of art collectors. Most of the time her joy at talking about art was clear, but when the male she was with left to speak to someone else, he could see her discomfort.

It was subtle, but her spine had gone rigid even as she laughed politely at something a mated couple said to her.

As he watched her, he flashed back to their first meeting and wanted to ram his big dumb dragon head into the side of a mountain and let the rubble bury him for a century.

He'd been in the training center with his friend and fellow warrior Octavia watching over a new group of trainees in the arena below them. Their training center was built into the side of a mountain that gave off a natural gas that overwhelmed everything else to the point that their ability to scent an attacker was moot.

Which was part of the appeal. He trained these males and females without one of their senses, so they relied on other instincts, not their inborn scenting skill. It made them even deadlier.

*"Lady Anastasia thinks you're being too hard on this group," Octavia murmured, coming to stand next to him as he surveyed the group of twelve in hand-to-hand combat. "I heard she was complaining to Starlena."*

*"That's because she's a pampered moron." It was also because her son was one of his newest trainees. Normally they only took in clan-less dragons to train. Dragons with no family and no wealth. Luckily, Anastasia's son was holding his own and would hopefully make a skilled assassin one day.*

*"No arguments from me." Octavia shook her head. "Who the fuck does she think she is anyway? Going to Starlena about this? She shouldn't even know what we're doing here."*

*He grunted in agreement. And the truth was, the female didn't know a thing about what they did or how they trained. She was simply a wealthy dragon who was worried about her son. Something he could possibly appreciate, but no one told him how to train his people. His training meant they had a chance at survival when they infiltrated other realms. And it was how this realm remained safe, secure. There was no room for weakness in his warriors.*

*"Next she'll want us to recruit those new humans in the territory." He still couldn't believe Starlena was on board with humans living in the Nova realm.*

*Octavia snickered next to him. "Can you imagine?"*

He grunted again. "Goddess no. They shouldn't even be allowed in the realm. Weak and pathetic, all of them."

At a gasp, he turned around and realized that a petite female was staring up at him. With emerald green eyes, long auburn hair and pretty pink cheeks, she was most definitely human.

And with one look, he was also certain that she was his... mate.

# CHAPTER 3

"Where did you go?" Mia kept her smile in place as she gritted out the question.

Jonothon placed a full flute of something very similar to champagne—with a little more of a kick—in her hands, and grinned. "Oh, just flirting with a couple vampires."

She blinked. "Vampires?"

"The queen has graciously allowed a handful of outsiders in for a fortnight. Art lovers mostly."

It wasn't out of the ordinary, not since the Nova realm had opened themselves up to the outside world. It was the only reason Mia was here. But the mention of vampires made her heart stutter—and not in a good way. She had vampire friends, but... she mentally shook herself. She was just letting the past get in her head because this was such a big night. "So tell me about these vampires."

"I might have a date later tonight. Or two."

She nudged him with her hip as they came to stand in front of a gorgeous sculpture of a dragon emerging from a nearby lake. The little flecks of "water" on the dragon scales looked so real shimmering under the gallery lights. "You're so talented," she murmured.

"And we're already friends so you don't have to butter me up."

She laughed lightly. "I'm serious. I'm so in awe of your work."

He cleared his throat, his cheeks flushing pink. "Coming from you, that means a lot. Thank you." He cleared his throat again, his expression turning pointed as he glanced behind her. "And someone has been watching you all night."

Surprised, she turned and found Tiber talking to a tall female who she guessed was likely a warrior given her more casual garb. And he wasn't even glancing in her direction. She turned back to Jonothon. "Shut your beautiful mouth." She knew he was simply messing with her. Tiber couldn't stand her or humans in general, and fine, she'd made her opinion on him clear to her friend. So now Jonothon liked to mess with her whenever the big dragon was lurking around. "I can't believe he's even here," she muttered. This didn't seem like his kind of hangout.

Then she felt guilty for the mean thought. Everyone could appreciate art, no matter where they came from. Something she understood more than most.

As she and Jonothon talked, two slim, definitely vampire, males approached, looking at her friend with clear interest.

"Your two dates?" she whispered.

"Hmmm." A non-response as he kissed her cheek. "I'm going to dip out early, but I'll see you tomorrow. Love you."

"You too." She tried to keep her voice light, but her only friend here, her crutch, was gone. And there was nothing keeping her from sneaking out too. You know, except *guilt*.

Jonothon was from here, knew his place in this territory was secure. She was still an outsider. Something she was reminded of every day in this place of magic and wonder. She was a human and felt like she had to fight for her place here.

Feeling awkward, and wanting to get away from Tiber, she started to walk around the giant sculpture, but froze when she saw *him*. Her ex.

Ice slicked her veins as she stared at his hard, handsome profile. Without thinking, her body simply moving, she ducked back behind the sculpture.

She could actually feel her anxiety kicking in, her heart rate galloping out of control. The walls were closing in on her, everyone's voices starting to blend into a cacophony of clashing noises.

She knew she had to leave. He could *not* see her. She wanted to know why he was here, but her main priority was getting the hell out of here before he approached her. Barely aware of her feet moving, she headed toward the nearest exit and found herself almost slamming into a wall of muscle.

Tiber.

Of course.

Because the goddess or whoever was having fun with her.

His amber eyes were filled with concern as he looked down at her. That sight brought her out of her spiral as his big hands landed on her bare arms. And his touch... oh, that could not be a spark. Nope.

"Are you okay?" His rumbly voice was... ugh. Wonderful.

"Fine," she rasped out and shoved her drink into his chest, basically forcing him to take it before she ducked away from him and through the nearby exit.

Never before had she been so thankful for the cold, fresh air as she stepped onto the cobblestone street. Or alley, she guessed, since it was a side exit.

Trying to steady her breathing, she carefully walked in her kitten-heeled shoes toward the main street that ran along the middle of the town. She'd worn flats and carried her current shoes in a little bag she'd left in the curator's backroom. She'd also left her coat there, but no way was she going back inside to retrieve it.

"What's wrong? Has someone insulted you?" Tiber's deep voice so close behind her made her jump. And squeak. Which was just plain embarrassing.

"Don't sneak up on me!" Her voice shook.

He held up his palms. "I thought I made a lot of noise. I wasn't trying to scare you."

She hated that he actually looked concerned. "Are you following me?"

"Yes."

She blinked at the unexpected answer. "Oh. Well, you don't need to. I'm fine." She still risked a quick glance over her shoulder to see if anyone else had come out with him. Thankfully, it was just Tiber. Words she'd never thought she would think.

He simply frowned at her, all tall and intimidating. "Did someone touch you?" he asked even as she walked away from him.

Slowly. Stupid shoes.

"No one touched me." Her teeth chattered slightly, and she wasn't sure if it was from the cold or knowing that her ex was in the vicinity. Because there was no doubt that it was him. He was an art lover and an extremely wealthy vampire, so it wasn't out of the realm of possibility that he'd been invited with whatever group was there. But his presence worried her.

"Was it Jonothon?" he growled.

She stared up at him. "What? No. He's my friend."

Tiber simply grunted and she realized that he was still walking with her as they stepped onto the main road. There were a handful of people wearing dresses and exquisite tunics standing outside the gallery, but none were her ex.

"You can go back to the party. I'm fine now. Just got a little overwhelmed with all the noise."

"You are a terrible liar."

"I was overwhelmed." Did she sound defensive? At least her heart rate was back to normal. Well, normal-ish. When she was next to Tiber, she was out of sorts in general, but she was still shocked at having seen her ex.

"That I believe. But it is not why you are leaving. If you'll tell me who offended you, I'll whittle down their femur bones until they're utensil-sized and stab—"

"Tiber!" She wasn't sure if she should be horrified or laugh. He couldn't be serious, right? That was when she saw the glint in those amber eyes. "You're messing with me?"

He simply grinned and oh, no one should be allowed to look that good when they smiled. Everything about him was hard and deadly, but that smile...

Frowning, she glanced away. He hated humans. She couldn't forget that. "Why are you following me home?" She glanced around the quiet street as they headed back to the artist's enclave she currently called home. It had become a real home in the last few months in a way she'd never imagined.

"Starlena asked me to keep an eye on you."

Ah, there it was. And it made sense. He would only have agreed to escort her if Starlena requested it. She shivered again and to her surprise, Tiber draped something over her shoulders. Some sort of sash thing that had been around his tunic.

"You don't—"

"I can hear your teeth chattering." His tone was dry.

And fine, he was right, she was freezing. "Thank you." The wrap thing smelled amazing too but she resisted the compulsion to bury her face in it. Instead, she wrapped it tighter around her shoulders, thankful for the warmth.

The rest of the walk was awkward and silent, so that was fun. She couldn't stop the sigh of relief when they finally made it to the enclave she lived in. Which was really a bunch of mountain chalets built in a circular shape, with pathways connecting all of them. Most of the artists lived with their mates or a roommate if they chose.

She'd taken a solitary chalet because she valued her privacy and hadn't been sure about potential roommates when she'd arrived. Plus, her cat Neptune could be temperamental, and she'd been worried he wouldn't get along with shifters. He was usually playful and sociable, but he'd had weird reactions to some shifters. Thankfully, her worries had been for naught, and he got along with all her friends.

The homes were built with incredible insulation, lots of glass for natural light and she wasn't sure of the other building materials because they weren't the same as in the human realm. And the big difference was that the homes were more rounded and most of the roofs opened up for a dragon to fly out if needed. She'd never had that particular need, but she loved that half the roof was glass. She felt like she was outside even when she was in the warmth and working.

"Oh, you don't have to walk me all the way to..." She trailed off when it was clear that he was ignoring her.

She also noticed that he'd matched his stride to her much slower one. And he hadn't made any impatient sounds or acted like she was too slow. It surprised her considering what he thought of humans. He must be on his best behavior for Starlena.

"This is me," she said as they approached one of the homes. She'd left a few of the magic-fueled lights on inside so there was a warm, inviting glow waiting for her. When she opened the door, he once again surprised her—by brushing past her and stepping inside as if he had every right to enter her residence.

"What the heck are you doing?" she demanded, slipping off the heels by the door before following after him.

"You stank of fear when you ran out of the gallery. Someone clearly scared you and since you won't tell me about it, I'm going to check your place and make sure that there is no threat here. I want you to sleep soundly tonight."

Oh. "I have a cat," she called out as he hurried up her stairs.

He made a grunt of acknowledgement but didn't slow down. She blinked as he moved through her place with efficiency, not even bothering to glance at her as he disappeared into her bedroom.

She was tempted to follow after him, but started a pot of tea instead, knowing that Neptune was likely hiding from their interloper. She might not care for Tiber, but right now he was actually making her feel better. It didn't matter that Starlena had clearly ordered him, she was still on edge and him checking out her place went a long way in easing that punch of fear from earlier.

As she pulled down two mugs he strode back in, looking a little ready to murder something. Alarm punched through her. "Did you find something?"

"No." And he looked annoyed by that.

"Isn't that a good thing?"

"Of course."

"Then why do you look like you want to punch something?" Or burn it to a crisp.

He looked around the kitchen and connected living room with something akin to curiosity in his gaze as he said, "Because you won't tell me what the threat is, and I was hoping to kill something tonight."

She blinked, unable to stop her mouth from falling open. He was joking again, right?

He looked at her and shrugged. "I will find out."

"Is this a dragon thing? The whole curiosity thing?" She poured a mug for him and slid it across the little island.

Staying on the other side—she needed distance from the big dragon thank you very much—she poured herself a mug and inhaled the hints of lavender.

"It's a Tiber thing," was all he said as he took a tentative sip of the tea.

And she had no idea how to respond. This whole situation was weird.

As he sat there, he glanced down and that was when she heard the purring.

"Oh, that's my—"

He leaned down and before she realized what was happening, he was sitting there holding her cat and drinking her tea. "This is delicious, thank you."

She stared as her giant Maine Coon, a regal fluffball of smoky gray fur and green eyes, butted his head up against Tiber's chin and purred insistently.

"He likes when you scratch the top of his head," she muttered. Traitor.

Tiber cleared his throat as he began gently scratching the big baby. "Did you enjoy the auction? Before whatever happened to scare you?"

"I... did not really enjoy it," she said, finding herself being honest and she wasn't even sure why. She didn't want to make small talk with him, but she also didn't want to lie for reasons beyond herself. Besides, she was pretty sure he'd be able to tell if she wasn't truthful.

Dragons and other shifters could scent it, she'd been told. And... her cat seemed to like him. That counted for something. "I'm grateful that so many people came to see my work and all the other artists involved, but I get anxious being around so many people."

"You're very talented," he said in response. "It's no surprise that so many came to buy your work."

"Thank you." A compliment from human-hater Tiber? She didn't know what else to say after that. Seeing her ex there in the Nova realm had ripped away her sense of self, her sense of safety, if she was being honest. She just wanted to be alone right now.

After a few more seconds, Tiber set his mug down. "I'll leave you be. But I'll be sleeping out in the adjoining area between the chalets in my dragon form. I don't want you to be startled if you look out your window and see a dragon."

"You don't have to stay. That's... ridiculous. I'm fine."

"I am a ridiculous dragon."

She blinked at him. "You can't just agree with me!"

He shrugged, giving her the hint of a mischievous grin and for a moment she saw his dragon looking back at her, his eyes amber and gold and oh god, she desperately wanted to paint him. All of him.

Worse, she was pretty sure the beast looking back at her knew it.

# CHapTer 4

Tiber stripped off his tunic, neatly folded it and placed it on a stone bench. There was plenty of seating in between the artists' residences and he'd found a perfect spot to shift and still be close to Mia's house.

He heard her before she spoke, but he stilled, waiting as she moved in behind him. He'd scared her before even though he'd made plenty of noise when he'd come up behind her in that alleyway. It was clear he'd have to be careful not to startle her.

"Tiber?"

He turned, saw that she was still in her dress and she looked nervous. Unlike the fear from before, this was a different scent. Tart and wild. Frustration and nerves, he thought. "Yes?"

Her mouth did a sort of pouty thing and he wanted to get on his knees and worship her, but he remained still as she clearly battled with something. Finally, she cleared her throat. "This is sort of annoying, but Jonothon isn't here, and everyone is still at the auction... And I can't get the ties free." She pointed behind herself, then turned around, giving him her smooth, creamy back.

The dress dipped low, exposing an expanse of pale skin he wanted to caress and kiss. And there were indeed thin, fine straps tied across her back in a couple places.

"I think he knotted them, but I can't tell."

"He?"

"Oh. Jonothon. He helped me secure it earlier."

Tiber only realized he was growling when she turned her head to look at him. "Is something wrong?"

So many things. But he simply shook his head. "I can untie the straps. It'll just take a minute."

Nodding, she turned back around and he had to take a minute before he started working on the top strap. Otherwise, he would tear them right off.

*Mate*, his dragon purred.

You are mistaken.

*No, you are stupid.*

I'm not having this conversation again. A delicate human is not our mate. When would his dragon ever listen?

*Wrong. Mate. And she smells good. It's too bad she doesn't shift because I could easily woo her. Unfortunately, she's stuck with you. Which means we'll never be mated and will be alone forever. I'm going to die alone, pining for a mate right in front of us.*

"Oh sweet goddess, shut up!"

Mia whipped around and he almost ripped the tiny strap. "Excuse me?"

"I... wasn't talking to you."

She blinked, then frowned. "Oookay. Who were you talking to?"

"My dragon."

Her eyes grew even wider, but she simply turned around.

*Now you've done it. I take back what I said. I can probably convince her so just shift and—*

Shut. Your. Mouth.

His dragon grumbled but at least went blessedly silent.

Tiber skated his fingers against Mia's back as he worked on the silky material. Did he take longer than necessary simply so he could bask in her orange blossom scent? Absolutely. Did he enjoy feeling her soft skin against his fingertips? Goddess above, he would give up his hoard to touch her again.

When he was finished, he cleared his throat. "I'm done."

"Thank you." She didn't turn around as she hurried back to the house, and he figured he'd blown things even more with her.

If that was even possible.

Sighing, he finished stripping and shifted, the ancient magic coursing through him soothing as his beast finally took over.

Then he scooted closer to Mia's house.

If anyone thought to bother her, he would simply eat them for a snack.

*** 

Mia stayed in the shadows of her house behind one of the curtains, but was pretty sure that the giant, gorgeous beast outside could see her anyway.

Probably because Neptune was sitting on the windowsill shamelessly watching him. Not that she could blame her baby.

Tiber's dragon was gorgeous.

There was no other word for him.

Or maybe there were a lot of words for him, but gorgeous, stunning... oh god, she wanted to paint him as he was. Something she could never, ever tell him.

The gold-amber of his scales shimmered under the moonlight in a truly magical sight. A full silvery moon hung in the sky and each time clouds drifted in front of it, it was like he retreated into the shadows, his scales becoming almost impossible to see.

She wanted to step back out into the cold to see if her eyes were playing tricks on her, but she was too nervous. Her understanding of dragon shifters was more than most humans, but there was still so much she needed to learn.

Because, apparently, Tiber talked to his dragon half? Out loud, it seemed.

And she knew how he felt about humans and figured that his dragon half would view her as a snack.

So she was going to stay inside... and simply watch the big animal slumber. Both her and Neptune.

His eyes finally drifted closed, but she was under the impression it wouldn't matter. That he would hear or scent any intruders.

That knowledge gave her the ability to finally slide into bed and close her eyes—Neptune didn't follow her. She didn't put thoughts of her ex completely out of her mind, but deep down, she knew Tiber wouldn't let anyone get inside her house.

Not even a charming vampire who was used to getting his way.

He might not like humans, but right now, Tiber had given her peace of mind. And that mattered.

# CHAPTER 5

*Dear Robin,*

*Last night I saw Charles at the auction I told you about. I don't know if I should say anything to anyone. He never hurt me, and I have no proof of anything but... I'm scared. And I need advice. I don't think he saw me, but he had to have seen my art at the show.*

*I have so many questions, but I'm scared to ask anyone who might know in case they decide I'm too much trouble and kick me out of the territory. It's probably just my anxiety rearing its ugly head, but I can't shake the thought that he's here because of me.*

*Oddly enough, that rude dragon Tiber walked me home last night and checked my place to make sure I felt safe. I don't know how I feel about that. I still remember his ugly words about humans, but he made me feel safe last night. He told me the reason he escorted me home was because he was ordered to, but I actually managed to sleep last night because of him.*

*Today, I'm going to try to find out more information about the newcomers and see if I can find out how long the vampires from Charles's coven will be staying. I'm hoping to find out without alerting anyone that I'm actually interested. Have you heard anything about his people since I've been gone?*

*I love and miss you and hope you visit soon.*

*Xo,*
*Mia*

# CHAPTER 6

Mia sealed her newest letter, then snuck a peek out the upstairs window from her bedroom. The sun had been up for an hour or so and Tiber was gone, of course. Even though she was warm inside, the sky was overcast and from her window she could see a snowcapped mountain in the distance and wondered if they'd get snow this week.

He'd stayed the night, she was sure of it. She'd seen him curled up outside right before sunrise. Neptune had stayed by the window all night watching him too. Seriously, her cat was being ridiculous.

Though she couldn't blame him. Seeing the gold-amber dragon still snoozing outside her home had made taking a shower and getting ready so much more peaceful. He'd been a soothing presence when her mind was full of chaos. Part of her had wanted to sketch the beast and save it for inspiration later, but had felt weird about doing so.

Once he'd woken, she'd planned to offer him tea and breakfast, but he was gone.

Just as well.

Last night was a fluke and they were *not* going to be friends.

Besides, she had things to do today, including figuring out (subtly) why her ex was in the Nova realm. Or more specifically, how long he was here for. She needed a game plan to avoid him if possible. He'd never physically hurt her, but he was manipulative and there was a darkness in him he'd shown to her after the breakup. He wanted to hurt her and those close to her—and he'd made sure she knew that he could.

If necessary, maybe she'd take Tiber up on that whole "whittle his femur bones down to chopsticks." Despite the heaviness on her chest, she snickered as she replayed his words, really hoping he'd been joking.

Once she'd fed Neptune and had gotten dressed, she grabbed her second favorite coat and stepped outside.

A large male wearing clothes similar to Tiber's—an open tunic secured with a large sash and loose pants and shoes made with leather and some kind of animal fur—stood up from one of the stone benches.

"Mia." He nodded politely at her.

"Ah, yes?"

"My name is Cyprus. Tiber asked me to escort you wherever you wanted to go today."

She blinked as she digested his words. "I appreciate it, but it's not necessary."

He shrugged. "Maybe not, but he requested it."

"Requested or ordered?" She slid her bag a little higher on her shoulder as she approached him.

"Either way, I value my life, so I will be your shadow. I'm good company, I promise."

This was beyond strange, but she could see the firm set of his jaw. This wasn't an argument she'd win. "I have a lot of errands to run."

"I can help you carry your stuff. I'm a wonderful assistant." He grinned at her, turning his hard, weathered face into something softer and mischievous.

Okay, well, at least he seemed nice. She found herself smiling back at him. "I'm sorry your day will be spent with me, but thank you."

"So why am I escorting you around, anyway?"

"Tiber didn't tell you?" she asked as they headed down the walkway that would lead to the main road. She waved at a few of her friends who were already out and starting their day.

"He simply said that if I wanted to retain my head, I would follow you around."

"Oh my god."

Cyprus laughed. "I'm jesting. And no, he didn't tell me, just asked me to keep you safe." The big male paused, glanced around the busy street. "Is someone threatening you?"

"No, of course not." But she couldn't stop the tightness in her chest at the knowledge that Charles was in the territory. It bothered her on a visceral level. He hadn't taken her breakup with him well.

At first, she'd thought he'd been fine, but then strange things had started happening. People she loved had started getting hurt—and he'd hinted that he'd been behind everything without actually admitting it. He'd been so careful but hadn't been able to hide himself from her. She'd seen the malice in his eyes. So she'd left, thinking it would eliminate the problem.

She'd been in the Nova realm for months, had found a home and according to her friends back in New Orleans, everyone was fine. Unharmed. She'd assumed that leaving had worked—out of sight, out of mind. He'd forgotten her.

"I can't imagine why Tiber wants you to shadow me," she added, not even believing the words herself. The scent of her fear must have been bad enough for the human-hating dragon to call in someone to watch her.

Cyprus didn't respond, but true to his word, he was more or less her shadow as they headed down the cobblestone street. In this realm, there weren't any motorized vehicles. What was the point when everyone here could fly? Instead, they relied on shifting and other magical means of travel. For the day-to-day stuff, people walked, rode bikes, or rode animals that looked similar to horses. The same animals also pulled carriages for larger traveling parties who weren't flying for whatever reason. The weirdest thing for her to adjust to was seeing the carriages that moved by magic alone.

"I heard the auction was busy last night," Cyprus said politely as they approached the now quiet gallery building.

She still needed to pick up her coat and shoes from last night. "It was. Did you attend?" Ooh, maybe he would be a good source of information for anything she'd missed after she'd run out of there.

"No, not my scene. But I heard Tiber purchased a couple pieces. Everyone is talking about it," he whispered almost conspiratorially.

She had a feeling this Cyprus liked to make mischief. She was also pretty sure she was going to like him. "Why are people talking about him buying art?"

He grinned down at her as they stepped into the gallery. "Because he paid an obscene amount—"

"Mia! My sweet girl!" Xenia ran the gallery and was tall even by dragon standards. She was a couple inches taller than Cyprus even, so she had to bend down to air kiss Mia. Her long white hair was in a braid woven through with little sprigs of a local fuchsia-colored flower that somehow bloomed even in winter.

She was what Mia imagined a real goddess looked like—stunning and larger than life in every way.

"I missed seeing you last night," Mia said, lightly embracing the woman she'd come to adore.

"I know, I was late and missed most of the auction, but Valentina is my hero." She nodded politely at Cyprus. "You're with Mia?"

"Yes," Mia said before he could tell her the real reason he was with her. She didn't want anyone to suspect that something was going on. No way did she want to be seen as a troublemaker. "He's running errands with me today."

"Ah, good man." She patted Cyprus's arm once then turned all her focus on Mia. "I'm guessing you're here to talk about your sales."

"Oh, actually I left my coat and shoes here last night," she said on a laugh, hoping it didn't sound forced. "I was so distracted. I can't believe I left my things."

"Ah, I knew those must have been yours, the coat thing is so small. Plus, it smells like you. Come, come." She motioned them back through the gallery where two people were currently wrapping up different sculptures and paintings.

"It looks like last night was successful," Mia said as they stepped into her office.

"Beyond so. And you and Jonothon were my biggest stars. You both sold out and now you both have requests to do commission work." She plucked up Mia's coat and Cyprus took it when she went to give it to Mia.

"Sold out?" She tried to stay cool, but who was she kidding? This was amazing.

"Oh yes, with demands for more, more, more. You are in high demand, my dear."

It seemed too good to be true, too surreal. She knew that was the anxiety talking, that voice in her head that loved to tear her down.

She glanced over at Cyprus who was gently folding up her long wool, eggplant-colored coat she'd brought from the human realm.

She'd had it since before The Fall and it was her absolute favorite since she'd bought it after her first real sale. It had been a splurge and one she'd never regretted.

Maybe Cyprus saw something on her face because he said, "I'll take care of it for you, unless you want to wear it?"

"I'm okay. And thank you." She was still reeling from the news of selling out.

Xenia cleared her throat. "Like I was saying, the McIlroy clan wishes to offer you a commission. They mentioned a year, but I already told them that would likely be too long for you. Yes?"

Mia nodded. It was definitely too long to commit to something like that. Too many unknowns. "I don't know how I feel about doing commission work when I haven't even been here that long."

"I can't tell if you're serious or trying to get a higher commission but either way, you're smart to say no to them the first time. They're going to go crazy if they can't have you." Xenia grinned at the prospect. "You need to make them work for your talent."

"If I did say yes—and it's a big if—I would need more details about my living situation, other expectations, payments, everything."

"Of course. I'm already creating something for you to look over. I take care of my people and no matter what, you'll have an out in the contract. You would be a contract employee and if you end up being unhappy, you get to walk away and they get to deal with it."

"That doesn't sound too bad then." She was still leaning toward no, but she would look at the proposed details anyway. Clearing her throat, she tried to sound casual. "So, there were some people from my realm here last night. Ah, a vampire coven I think?"

Xenia smiled and nodded. "Oh yes. They were mostly interested in sculptures and other mixed media, but one of them loved your work. He tried to buy a couple of your paintings but was outbid on all of them." She looked a little smug. "I was right to hold back some of your stuff because now you'll have more to show at the next auction."

Oh right, they were supposed to do one more showing at the end of the week. Mia's abdomen clenched at the thought. "Of course. I... wanted to ask if it was strictly necessary if I attend the other auction?"

"Ah... no. Buyers love to meet the creators, the 'genius' behind the work, but if you have something else to do then it's not necessary at all. If anything, your absence will probably drive up the prices even more." She waggled her finger at Mia. "You really do think like a dragon, and I love it."

Mia laughed lightly. She'd come to learn that dragons were obsessed with getting the best deal and absolutely loved to hoard treasure. That little nugget wasn't just myth; dragons loved shiny things, sometimes to a ridiculous level.

"How long do you think the vampires will be in the realm?" She aimed for casual again, but could feel Cyprus watching her.

Damn it, she didn't need him running back to Tiber.

"They've been allowed to remain for the next fortnight, so they'll be here this week and the next. If the queen allows, they might stay longer, but she's being cautious with how long she allows outsiders to stay." Then Xenia placed a gentle hand on her arm. "You are excluded from that. In fact, I'm certain she wants you to stay permanently."

"Oh. Well, I love it here." Mia was too afraid to get her hopes up that she could call this place home. Permanently.

"Oh, good," Xenia breathed out in relief. "I'll courier you information about your sales and the details of the proposed contract by the end of the day or tomorrow at the latest. I hope you're taking the day to enjoy yourself. You've earned it."

"I am, thank you." Today was more about errands, but Xenia was right, she should relax.

After more air kisses, she found herself outside with Cyprus once again, breathing in the crisp air.

"Seems as if you might find a permanent home here, human."

She glanced up at him in surprise. "I just might, dragon."

He let out a startled laugh, drawing some looks from those on the street. "Apologies."

"No need."

"You're the first human I've ever met," he added. "It just slipped out."

"Am I really the first human you've met?" She motioned which direction she wanted to go and he fell in step with her.

She noticed that people seemed to automatically move out of his way. Something she found interesting. Even among dragons, people gave this guy a wide berth. It was the same with Tiber.

*Stop thinking about him*, she ordered herself.

"Indeed. And I've seen your work—Tiber spoke of your talent but I wasn't sure I believed him until I saw two of your paintings back there."

"Tiber talked about my work?" She couldn't hide the surprise in her voice.

"Oh yes. When he threatened to remove my head from my body this morning, he mentioned that if the realm lost such a talent under my watch, the queen would likely slice off my head if he didn't do it first."

She snorted. "Now I know you're exaggerating."

He snickered slightly and she saw that hint of mischief again. Oh, he was definitely a troublemaker. "Ah, the market," he said as she stopped at the next alleyway. "One of my favorite places."

"I wasn't kidding about running errands. Are you sure you're up to carrying all my things?" Normally she had her packages delivered but she figured he was big enough to haul everything and she was going to take advantage.

He flexed his arms once for her, grinned.

And she found herself laughing again.

# Chapter 7

Valentina gave Tiber an assessing look before she turned back to the head chef and barked out orders about the evening's meal. It had taken a while, but he'd finally hunted her down. An almost impossible feat in a castle that stayed busy all the time.

The chef simply nodded at Valentina, then turned to his staff and ordered them to join him.

Valentina motioned for Tiber to follow her. "Come. We can talk somewhere quieter."

"It's fine. I know you're busy. Thank you for making time for me." He could be diplomatic when he needed to be. He preferred battle and having a clear target, but there were times when he could put on a polite, civilized face for the world.

She gave him another one of those assessing looks. "There are no refunds on your art."

"I know that. That is not why I'm here." He would never return Mia's art. They were his treasure. He was even sharing it with his guard so they could all see her talent. It went against his nature not to hoard it, but her work deserved to be displayed for everyone.

Valentina was still eyeing him, and he couldn't get a read on her expression. "I saw you leave with Mia last night. If you insulted that sweet human—"

"Goddess," he growled. "I had planned to be more subtle, but I guess I don't need to be. Someone scared her last night."

"Who?" Valentina's entire demeanor changed, her dragon in her gaze as she turned to face him. As usual, she had blades strapped to her thighs and looked ready to cut someone's heart out. It was one of the reasons he liked her.

"I don't know. But something or someone scared her, and she ran out. She tried to cover it up, but her fear was thick. I simply followed and escorted her home." He would have done more if she'd allowed him, but at the moment she barely tolerated his presence.

"Fear?"

"I think I know how to detect scents," he said dryly. But it bothered his dragon that Mia had been scared.

She sniffed once, but her gaze was back to normal as she turned away from him and headed down a long corridor.

He kept pace with her through the maze of corridors until they were finally in her office. "Why do you not have a larger space?" He paced the office in ten long strides, frowned as he took in the scant decor. She had a lot of natural light and it was in a good location as it was close to the queen, the kitchen, and the main hub of activities, but someone of her station could ask for something more than this...closet.

"If I have a bigger space, it will encourage people to linger." Her tone was dry as she rummaged through a set of files on her desk. "And this is where I work, not my home," she added as she pulled out a handful of papers. She held them out to him. "This is a list of everyone who attended last night, including outsiders."

"You're just giving me this information?"

"You're Starlena's most trusted... I don't actually know what your title is. But I know she trusts you, and that's good enough for me."

"What do you want me to do with this?"

She lifted an eyebrow. "You want instructions?"

"No. I just want to make sure we're on the same page."

"If someone is threatening one of our own, *handle* it. I micromanage far too many people. You are not one I'm worried about. If there's a problem, make it go away."

Taking the papers, he left without another word. That had gone far easier than he'd expected. He'd thought he'd have to involve Starlena, despite that his ranking in the castle was likely as high as Valentina's.

Though if someone had indeed threatened Mia, he would be handling it with or without anyone's permission. He didn't need any to take care of his future mate. But it would make things easier. He read over the names of the outsiders on the list as he made his way to the nearest exit.

He had to stop by the training arena first but after that, he would return to check on Mia and Cyprus. He'd chosen Cyprus to watch over Mia today and hoped the other male didn't scare her too much.

The deadly warrior was known for his skill in beheading others in close quarters, not his friendly disposition. He also wasn't a flirt, something that couldn't be said for half of his guard.

***

"Oh sweet goddess, you're ridiculous!" Mia laughed as Cyprus balanced his body weight on one hand, showing an impressive amount of strength.

"I think this is what your fans truly want. And I'm willing to pose for as long as it takes."

She threw a blackberry at him and to her surprise, he jumped onto both feet and caught the fruit midair in one hand. Then he took a bow before he ate it.

She snickered as she continued organizing her paintbrushes. "I'm looking to paint a dragon—in shifted form. Not... whatever that was."

"I think my scales might be too sensitive to paint."

Blinking, she looked up at him and realized he was joking.

"Ha, ha. You know what I meant." She eyed him for a moment as he grazed on the fruit plate she'd set out.

They'd returned to her studio about an hour ago and true to his word, he'd carried all her bags. Now she was cleaning up her studio because she'd been so manic before the auction and hadn't had time to put everything back in its place. Not to mention she had to replace all the paint she'd gone through. "I know you were joking, but are scales sensitive? I always thought they were like diamonds. Or rocks, I guess." She paused. "Is that rude to ask?" There were some unspoken rules in the supernatural world and she tried not to break any of them.

"Not rude at all. And no, they're not sensitive. They're like armor—" He straightened suddenly, his gaze shooting toward the entrance like a laser. His entire body was on alert.

She froze, wondering if she should be worried but then Tiber strode in, a scowl on his face. He glanced at her, his expression unreadable, then strode up to Cyprus where they did that warrior clasp.

"No issues, sir." Cyprus's words were clipped, his tone neutral. So unlike the relaxed male who'd been with her today.

Tiber simply nodded. "You can leave."

She stepped forward, frowning at Tiber. "Cyprus has been wonderful today." And he deserved a thank you. She looked at the other dragon.

"Thank you for keeping me company."

"Of course." He gave her a short bow, then said, "It was my pleasure. And I know what I said before, but it would be my honor to pose for you in the future."

"Thank you. I would love that."

Tiber clapped Cyprus on the shoulder and the other dragon bowed again before leaving.

"You were kind of rude to him," she said to Tiber once they were alone.

Tiber stared down at her, blinked. "I was rude?"

"He was with me all day on your orders, and you didn't even thank him."

Another blink. "He's one of my men. He was following my orders."

"So... he doesn't need thanks?"

"No."

She frowned and turned away from him to return to her brushes. They were in complete disarray. "So why did you have him watch me all day? I mean, I think I know, but we need to talk about this." He'd just made decisions without consulting her, which fine, was fair considering her ex. But still, she wanted some input.

"What is there to talk about? Someone scared you enough that I could scent it out of all the other scents in that gallery last night. That's not simply being worried about something. You are afraid and until I know why, you will have someone with you at all times." His words were hard, leaving no room for any discussion.

"Just like that?" She looked up from her brushes to find him looking around in curiosity.

Her space wasn't huge, but it was tall with windows everywhere and so much natural light, creating the perfect place for her to work. Once it was tidy and organized again, she could function.

"Yes." He cleared his throat and looked at her again. And this time she definitely saw the dragon peering back at her. "And if you want to paint a dragon, you can paint me, not Cyprus."

She barely resisted the urge to let her mouth fall open. "I will keep that in mind." It was the most diplomatic thing to say to him.

Of course, she wanted to paint him—despite what he'd said about humans. She'd seen his dragon last night and he was gorgeous, all sleek, golden power. He'd looked magnificent simply curled up in the grass. She could only imagine how gorgeous he would be in flight, the sun at his back. And fine, she was also intrigued at the idea of painting this male that people talked about in whispers.

He didn't seem to like her answer, but then said, "I have a list of everyone who was at the auction last night, including some individuals from your realm."

"Oh." Dread curled tight inside her, but she ignored it.

"If you tell me who scared you, I can make them go away." He said the words patiently.

"Go away?" She wanted to make sure she understood him correctly. And that he didn't mean murder.

But he paused far too long before answering. "I will make them leave the realm." His tone made it sound a lot like "bury them in a deep pit."

"Are you lying to me?"

She could see a battle going on in his amber eyes as he weighed his words. "I can't fully answer without knowing how bad this threat is."

"There is no threat," she murmured. Nothing that she could prove, anyway. Just a gut feeling that her ex had meant her harm. But he'd never physically hurt her, something she kept reminding herself of. But she swore he'd burned down her sister's garden and greenhouse, even if she couldn't prove it.

Tiber closed his eyes for a long moment. "Fine. What time would you like to leave this evening?"

"For what?"

"The festival. Xenia told me that you would be attending tonight."

"You spoke to Xenia?"

He nodded.

"Ah, I had planned on leaving in an hour or so. I still need to shower and get ready though."

"I'll escort you back to your place then."

"You don't have to do that." But she knew he wasn't listening at all.

"You'll love the street vendors," he said instead. "They have all the food you can imagine and then some."

There was real pleasure on his face as he spoke about the food and now, she was quite sure she'd pegged him wrong. Not totally, but there was more to this male than she'd originally assumed. Maybe she was a little biased since discovering he was a fan of her art and had actually purchased some pieces, but he was still here, trying to keep her safe. "You like the festivals?"

He shrugged and walked out with her into the waning sunlight. "I attend some years."

"What's your favorite type of art medium?" She might have her opinions about this big male, but he was worried about her safety simply because he'd smelled her fear, even though he disliked humans. And that counted for a lot. Maybe it was because of Starlena, but he still wanted to keep her safe.

She was so used to worrying about her family, her sister, and at one point, her mother. She'd always been the caretaker and now that someone was looking out for her, she wasn't sure how to react. But she wanted to get to know him better. To give him a chance.

"Ah, paintings."

Hmm. Why did he have to look so... striking? Everything about him was dark and dangerous and fine, gorgeous. He would make a perfect subject to paint. "Were you serious about posing for me? For a painting?"

He cleared his throat. "If you wish."

"I think I do wish." And she wouldn't be selling any paintings of him. Nope, those would be for her eyes only.

# CHAPTER 8

Tiber tried not to stare at Mia as they made their way to the festival. Each day this week there was something she had to attend—and he didn't like her being so exposed.

Not when there was something going on—a threat she refused to voice aloud. He wanted to simply order her to tell him.

But even he knew that was not the way to go.

"It's so beautiful out here." Her eyes lit up with joy as they reached the courtyard where thousands of magically lit bulbs floated over the party. "It's like the bazaar during the day, but on steroids."

He wasn't certain what steroids were—sometimes there wasn't always a translation—but he could guess from context. He simply nodded.

As part of the week-long festivities, tonight's was what she said, a bazaar. All artists, from someone with Mia's talent to those who created everyday items to sell. There were also street vendors and dancing—essentially it was a giant party.

As if dragons needed a reason to party.

At least it wasn't formal, and unlike the evening before, the people attending weren't the wealthiest in the realm. To be fair, he was wealthy, but only because he was ancient and he hoarded his treasure like... well, the dragon that he was.

And at that thought, he glanced at Mia again. She was the real treasure. Not that he could actually say that to her.

But at least she seemed to be tolerating him. *Maybe* even more than that. Or perhaps that was wishful thinking on his part.

"Mia!" Cyprus stepped out from behind two food vendors, a big smile on his face. Then he pulled her into a giant hug that had her laughing, the sound literal music to his dragons' ears.

He would have to remember to wipe that smile off Cyprus's face later.

"Tiber." Cyprus clapped him on the shoulder with a bone-rattling grip and pulled him into a hug.

Ah, his friend had gotten into his cups. Still, his dragon was right at the surface, dangerously close to coming out to play. And by play, his dragon wanted to rip the face off anyone who got too close to Mia. Even Cyprus.

*It is an acceptable courting gesture.* His dragon's tone was imperious.

It most definitely was not. Tiber ignored his dragon and nodded at Cyprus. "I see you're enjoying yourself."

"Indeed. This is one of my favorite weeks of the year." He smiled pleasantly as he looked between the two of them.

"Mia." A female he vaguely recognized approached them, hugged Mia with the same exuberance as Cyprus, then hustled her over to a nearby table next to one of the food vendors.

Cyprus's expression turned more serious once she was out of earshot. "Have you discovered anything about who is bothering her?"

His old friend had told him that she'd seemed particularly curious about the vampires visiting the realm. "Not yet, but I've sent someone to keep an eye on the vampires." The coven in the territory wasn't scheduled to attend these festivities at least. They were involved in some type of negotiation for trade.

"Who'd you send?"

"Octavia."

Cyprus nodded. "Good choice."

"Thank you for your approval," he said dryly.

The warrior gave him a surprised look, then grinned. "Ah, this is because I hugged her, yes?"

He glanced over to where Mia was currently talking to a handful of females who looked as delicate as she was. A couple humans, Tiber thought, but also some other types of shifters. Not dragons, that much he was almost certain of. They were all simply too short. There were, of course, exceptions to that rule (one of the realms' princesses was as small as a human) but he didn't recognize those females, so it was a safe assumption they weren't dragons.

Tiber lifted a shoulder. "Maybe you should keep your hands to yourself."

"And if I don't?" Cyprus was full-on grinning now. Obnoxious asshole.

He looked closely at his friend. "How much have you had to drink tonight?"

"Not enough. But I'll keep my hands to myself. Probably." He grinned, clapped Tiber on the shoulder once again before he sauntered off and blended into the growing crowd.

What the fuck had gotten into his friend? Tiber shook his head and took in the rest of the scene, not surprised to see Starlena arriving. But he was stunned to see her mate, Bodhin, with her.

He had the same regal bearing as Starlena, but there was something almost otherworldly about the ancient male that Tiber's dragon was very, very aware of. He was certain it was the male's age (which no one knew). He had silvery gray hair, just as Starlena did, given their age. But his eyes were a dark blue with flecks of silver in them. They were so very 'other' even for dragons. There was no way this male could pass as human or anything other than what he was.

Tiber bowed ever so slightly as the couple approached, but Starlena waved him off.

"Stop with that nonsense."

Yeah, that wasn't happening. The two were royalty, but it wasn't that. They were a true power and had protected, bled for, and destroyed for the kingdom in ways most people in the territory would never know.

"It's a pleasure to see you both out," he said, looking between the two of them.

Bodhin simply nodded.

"I heard the auction was quite the success—and that your little human was the star." Starlena grinned smugly at him.

His instinct was to tell her that Mia wasn't his human, but his dragon half told him to shut the fuck up. "The auction was indeed successful, but something odd is going on."

"I've already spoken to Valentina." Starlena pitched her voice low as she glanced around, making sure no one was close enough to overhear.

Of course, she had.

No one was paying them any attention. "I'm taking care of it."

She nodded as if she expected nothing less. "I have no doubt. We're actually here because I wanted to speak to you. Bodhin and I are leaving at first light. There's an issue in the western territory we've been asked to check into."

He straightened slightly, going on alert. "A threat? What do you need? I will go with you." Because if the queen had asked her parents to look into something, it could be a true threat. The kingdom hadn't been under siege in over a century, but everyone here remembered the last time they were attacked.

The bloodshed. The loss. The dragonlings who'd died.

He gritted his teeth, unable to dwell on the senseless violence.

It would never happen again, not under his watch.

Bodhin's quiet voice made him go still. "No. Your place is here."

Tiber glanced at him. The ancient male was looking off into the crowd, his expression one of contemplation, as if he wasn't seeing what was right in front of him. But Tiber had no doubt the male saw and would remember every single individual who passed in front of him tonight.

Tiber looked at Starlena, eyebrows raised.

She nodded in agreement with her mate. "Thank you for the offer, but you are needed here. You're one of the few people I trust to run our guard while I am gone. And if you must leave for any reason, you know who to leave in charge."

He nodded. Cyprus and Octavia worked well as a team and would keep the entire guard in line if he was called away. But he didn't like to leave when Starlena was away from the castle. It was part of his duty as general of their elite guard, one she'd recruited him for back when he'd been merely a warlord. Now he ran the day-to-day things including training and preparing for missions. He was too well known now to undertake any high-profile missions where he might be recognized, but he was training the newest generation of assassins and understood how important that was. "I'll keep the territory safe while you're gone. I won't leave."

Bodhin touched his arm gently, once again surprising Tiber. "Do not be so sure about that."

He looked at Starlena once again, as she usually translated for her mate who simply said what he wanted, and then that was that. But she just shrugged. The male had just told him that his place was here and now he was telling him not to be so sure about that? Tiber wondered if the ancient just liked to screw with people sometimes and speak in riddles.

Starlena's shrug was beyond infuriating—but not as infuriating as the sight of a male pulling Mia onto the nearby dance floor.

The band had started up again with a lively tune and all the dragons mingling and talking under the trees and lights started moving closer to the dance area, clapping, and cheering as everyone merged onto the dance floor.

His dragon reared up as he watched the other male pull her into his arms, and he stepped forward before he realized he was moving. He didn't bother saying anything to Starlena, belatedly realized he should have, but too late now.

It took restraint he'd never had to deal with before not to pound everyone who was in his way as he moved through the throng of mostly dragons. As he reached the side of the dance floor, he waited for his opening. As Mia and the male who was spinning her moved past him, he slid in between them, taking her into his arms.

He heard laughter behind him, assumed it was from the other dragon, but all his focus was on the breathless Mia in his arms.

She'd pulled her long hair into a braid, and it was coming loose, the wild auburn strands dancing around her face as she looked up at him in surprise.

He tried to smile at her, working muscles he hadn't in ages. She frowned up at him, but just as quickly, she laughed as he spun her, then pulled her back to him. Something in his chest loosened at the pure joy on her face, the sound of her laughter—the feel of her in his arms.

"You're a very good dancer. I'm not sure I even understand all the steps." She spoke in breathy laughs and he wanted to soak up every second of this moment.

Savor the feel of her in his arms. Her orange blossom scent was addicting as it wrapped around him.

He knew they were surrounded by people (something he normally hated) but everything around them was just background noise. She was the only one who existed. "I had to learn."

"Had to?" she asked as the music slowed.

And oh, he liked that. He pulled her a little closer, his dragon practically purring as their bodies slid together. "When I was just a young recruit, Starlena made all of us learn. Said it was a valuable tool to have in our arsenal." And she had been right, as she was about so many things.

He hadn't had to use that particular skill until about a hundred years after she'd forced him to learn, but it had helped him blend into enemy territory in the most unexpected of ways.

"It's hard to imagine you as a young recruit. How old were you when you first learned... if it's okay to ask that question? I'm a little fuzzy on the rules."

He shrugged. "I'm not quite sure how long ago." But it had been hundreds of years ago, and he didn't wish to remind her of their age difference. Not that it mattered in the slightest to him. But she was human, and he imagined she felt differently about such things.

He didn't wish to think of it at all. He'd already ruined their first meeting, and he wouldn't screw up again with her.

"Well, I'm impressed with your skills." She moved a little closer into his arms as the music slowed and when someone approached, clearly to cut in, he let his dragon show in his eyes. Though he resisted the urge to growl at them so that was something.

Tiber didn't think she noticed. "I'm impressed with your paintings," he said, trying to focus on the conversation at hand and not how good she felt in his arms.

How warm and alive and goddess, what he wouldn't give to bring her to climax right now. Maybe not *right* here, because he didn't share and would never let anyone else see her that way. But he wanted nothing more than to give her all the pleasure she deserved, to taste her sweetness.

Her cheeks flushed pink and sweet goddess, he had to look away. That was when he spotted another male moving toward them on the dance floor. His dragon roared to the surface again and the male smoothly headed in another direction when he saw the look in Tiber's eyes. By now everyone in the vicinity should know to stay away from them. He was staking a claim for all dragons to know that Mia was off limits.

"Impressed for a human?" Her tone was tart.

And he deserved it. He winced slightly. "You are talented. Period."

Her green eyes narrowed slightly at him. She started to say something, then yet another male approached. So apparently this dragon had a death wish.

"All her dances are taken," he growled at the well-dressed dragon he vaguely recognized as some royal asshole.

The male simply ignored him and smiled politely at Mia. "May I cut in?"

Oh, this one had balls. For now, anyway.

Mia smiled sweetly at him, and he tightened his grip on her. He knew she wasn't his, wasn't a possession, but he still wanted to keep her. His dragon half wanted to fly her into the mountains right this instant and add her to his hoard of treasure.

To his surprise, she shook her head. "Maybe later." Then she turned back to him as he subtly moved her closer to the edge of the dance floor. "I don't understand you at all, Tiber."

He loved when she said his name, had to bite back a groan of frustration and something else altogether. Need. Raw, desperate need for this sweet female with the big green eyes and so much talent he wanted to buy all her work and hoard it for himself. "What do you not understand?"

"You don't like humans."

"I never said—"

Her eyebrow arched.

"I might have said that. *Once*. And I tried to apologize but you didn't want to hear any of it."

"I still don't want to hear it because I don't believe you're sorry. I think you're sorry I overheard you and you were embarrassed." She sniffed imperiously, then something flashed across her face.

The same as the other night. Fear. She spotted someone behind him and moved in closer, clearly seeking protection.

He didn't care that she was using him as he held her close, inhaled her sweet orange blossom scent as she basically clung to him.

"I would like to leave," she whispered, her fingers digging into his back.

A dark, territorial protectiveness coiled inside him, ready to strike. "Whose head do I need to remove from their body?" He kept his voice pitched low.

She blinked up at him, stared for a long moment, then tightened her grip again as she gave him what he could only describe as a flirty smile. It was so at odds with her terrified scent. "No one," she clearly lied. "I would just like you to take me home now."

"Come on," he growled, ready to have her all to himself—even if he was ready to burn whatever or whoever was scaring her. "This way."

# CHAPTER 9

"This isn't the way to my house," Mia murmured.

"It's the way to mine." He tried to keep the gruffness out of his tone.

"We—"

"Are going to my place. And for the record, you didn't have to... flirt or whatever that was back there to get me to leave with you." His words came out a rough growl as he failed to keep his emotions in check. He'd loved having her wrapped around him, had imagined how she would feel skin to skin, but he didn't want her to feel like she had to pretend for him to keep her safe.

"I'm sorry," she whispered, her voice shaky.

Startled, he glanced down and realized how upset she was, the unshed tears in her eyes. He was so damn clumsy with her. Feeling lost, he patted her arm gently as they turned up a cobblestone path that would lead the way to his place.

She looked at him with a watery smile. "I'm sorry," she said again. "I was just scared." When he was about to say something (demand she name the threat), she seemed to read his mind. "I'll tell you everything when we get to your place. I would like privacy."

He nodded as they headed up the steep path. The most ancient, primitive part of him wanted to offer to carry her but knew she wouldn't appreciate it. She was clearly feeling vulnerable and terrified and even if they could get to the safety of his home much quicker if he carried her, he was well aware that she needed to feel some degree of control right now.

By the time they made it to his place, which was built into the side of the mountain that protected the back of the castle, he saw the surprise on Mia's face as she took in his home and the handful of others built right into the rockface.

"I've never seen anything like this."

"It goes back farther than you think." There were also multiple exits that would allow him or anyone with access to use them to escape. Centuries ago, he and the not-so-secret guard that Starlena oversaw had created an intricate cave system that allowed all of them to secretly leave the territory.

Technically, they could all leave using their natural born camouflage and simply fly away, but this was a failsafe for all of them and a way to ensure they could get dragonlings to safety if the kingdom ever came under attack again.

"It's so beautiful. I love how it's part of the mountain but can see how much natural light you must get during the day with all those windows."

He simply nodded and motioned for her to follow him. The door wasn't visible because he'd had it spelled with magic.

"Ah, Tiber..."

"Just trust me." He walked through the illusion, which was a simple boulder, and smiled at her gasp when he disappeared.

Then she stepped forward, hands out in front of her and grinned as she turned around in a circle. "Magic?"

"Most definitely."

She laughed lightly then said, "So is this the kind of magic that alerts you if you have intruders?"

He nodded, surprised by her question.

It must have shown on his face because she shrugged. "I grew up in the swamps. Even before supernaturals came out to the world—my world, I guess—I knew witches existed. Vampires too. Everything else was a big surprise though. I figured you'd have magical security here."

There was a bias against witches in the supernatural communities, and he'd never understood it. Though even as he had the thought, shame filled him at his own bias against humans. One he had moved past, but nonetheless, it shamed him that he'd been carrying around old prejudices and had insulted his future mate the first time they'd met.

The goddess was certainly laughing at him. Or as Starlena had once told him, the goddess believed in karma. He hated when Starlena was so obnoxiously correct.

"This is my home," he said as he pushed his front door open, a thick slab of stone he'd cut himself. "And to answer your question more specifically, my home was spelled by a witch. But you have access anytime you want, even when I'm not here." He'd added her to his list of approved people the moment he'd realized she was his mate.

It didn't matter that she'd hated him after that meeting, that they'd barely spoken. She would have access to his haven from now until the end of time.

"Oh... thank you." She sounded distracted as she looked around in definite curiosity. She stepped out of her soft-looking slippers and left them by the door.

He wanted to tell her that she didn't have to, but he found the sight of her brightly painted pink toenails adorable.

That was the correct word. Adorable.

He forced himself to turn away from her or all he would do was stare.

There was a large fireplace along one wall that also ran on magic (his dragonfire specifically), a lot of seating in the form of what were essentially overstuffed pillows, and little things he'd collected over the centuries. His sleeping space was directly above the living area and connected kitchen, though he did have two rooms for sleeping and storage as well for when people stayed with him.

Unlike most humans and indeed most dragons he knew who slept in beds, he had a dragon-sized mesh-style hammock stretched tight high up in his cave. It was anchored in four places and would only come down if the mountain itself did. His bed was also piled with interconnected cushions for maximum comfort. He often slept there in either human or dragon form, as it was large enough to hold his beast. And he liked sleeping so high in the air. It gave him the element of surprise if his home was ever invaded.

The plethora of magically spelled windows meant he got that perfect morning sunlight no matter where he was in his home.

He might have been an ancient warlord who came from the desert and had nothing but the clothes on his back when he started his long journey to becoming general of the elite guard, but he could admit that he loved his luxuries. He could live without them, of course, but as a dragon, he didn't want to.

"What's that up there?" She pointed to the bottom of the bed, which looked like nothing more than a tightly woven netting. From down below, it was impossible to see what the rest of it looked like.

"I sleep up there."

She blinked in surprise, but then nodded. "That's actually cool. This whole place is like a dream. I feel like I'm in a fairytale."

It was on the tip of his tongue to tell her to stay as long as she'd like (how about forever) but he knew how that would go over. Also, he needed to stay on track. Someone had scared her tonight and dealing with that threat was his main priority. Getting her naked and bringing her pleasure was a close second in his list of priorities. Very close.

"Did you get anything to eat at the bazaar?" he asked, even though he knew that she hadn't. He wanted to get her talking, relaxed. Because he needed the truth.

For her safety.

"No. I got so distracted." She shivered slightly and he wondered if he should increase the heat of his fireplace.

But then he had another thought and plucked one of his wraps off the back of a chair and handed it to her. "It's thick and will keep you warm. This way," he directed as she took it from him.

Normally he used the wrap to secure his weapons to his person, but he liked seeing it encompassing all of her. She'd wrapped it around her shoulders a couple times and was no longer shivering.

*And she'll smell like us,* his dragon added.

As if he hadn't had the same thought already.

"Sit." He motioned to the hardback chairs in his kitchen and opened his cooler, the equivalent of a human refrigerator.

Not exactly the same as the humans, as theirs were mechanical and his was magical, but the purpose was the same. He pulled out some cheese he'd recently bought from the market as well as some freshly baked bread he'd picked up that morning. Then he started a pot of jasmine and orange blossom tea.

"It's weird seeing you be so domestic." Her quiet voice cut through the air, a hint of amusement in her words.

"Why?" He turned to face her as the pot started to brew, then started cutting up the cheese and bread.

"I don't know. Because you're so..." She sort of motioned at him with her hands but didn't continue.

"I think the words you're looking for are impressive, strong and god-like. And we don't think of gods as eating or drinking," he said dryly.

She let out a startled laugh. "Oh my gosh, your ego! And, also, sort of. I don't know, you're a huge warrior dragon. I guess I just imagined you roaming the countryside snatching up little sheep or cows and eating them in one bite."

"So you've imagined me?" His dragon was incredibly pleased by that.

She laughed again, but the tenseness in her shoulders was long gone and goddess, he loved seeing her so relaxed.

He slid a plate of the cheese cubes and bread to her while he pulled out a small jar of jam. Her eyes lit up at the sight and he made a note to always be stocked with it.

She took a small spoon and slathered on jam as she looked anywhere but at him. "I guess I need to tell you about... what's bothering me."

He noticed how specific she was with her phrasing and wasn't sure what to make of it. "I want you to tell me about the threat."

Sighing, she looked at him. "I feel like I'm overreacting. I... I don't know how to get this out."

"Start at the beginning." He kept his voice pitched low and turned away from her to move the teapot off the stove. He hoped if he wasn't watching her, it would be easier for her to talk.

"I... before I moved here, I was involved with someone. A vampire."

Oh, he did not like that at all. The thought of anyone touching her... Not the point right now. He needed to listen. She was finally opening up.

*Do not fail her*, his dragon added. *But also, I will find her ex and eat him as a snack.*

"I don't know if this phrase will translate, but he basically love-bombed me. I know that gets thrown around a lot—where I'm from—and I can't believe I didn't realize it at first. I don't want to get into all the details."

"You can give me details." He slid the mug across to her, loved the way she faintly smiled as she inhaled. He also didn't want certain kinds of details—he was feeling murderous, and her ex was nearby. It should be easy enough to hunt him down and behead him. But only if he didn't mind causing a clash between realms.

"He was constantly praising me, telling me how talented I was, and within a week of dating he wanted to turn me into a vampire. I'm not sure how familiar you are with vampire customs, but that's ridiculously fast." She paused. "To be fair, I've had more offers to be turned, but usually by old vamps who want me to paint for them for like a decade." There was amusement in her voice as she shook her head. "They just like that I'm something new and shiny is all."

But then her expression sobered. "With Charles, it was different."

Charles. *Yes.* He finally had a name. He forced his expression to remain neutral, but she wasn't looking at him anyway. She was picking apart a slice of bread until it was nothing but little crumbles.

"In the beginning everything was fun and exciting and to him, I was perfect." There was a hint of bitterness in her voice. "Everything moved so fast, which normally would have been a red flag for me." She took a deep breath. "My mom was in her share of abusive relationships, and I stupidly thought that I'd see one coming. I thought I'd see the signs."

"That kind of shit sneaks up on you though," he murmured. He'd seen it time and again with people in his life.

She looked up at him in surprise, almost as if she'd forgotten he was there. He started to curse himself for speaking, but she gave him a ghost of a smile and nodded. "Yeah, exactly. He wanted to buy me things, to introduce me to all these important people, and he told me so much about him that he'd supposedly never told anyone else."

She rolled her eyes. "I didn't see it at the time, but he was trying to force a bond with me. Luckily, I guess, my sister knew the signs too. She was an outsider in our relationship and very gently pointed a few things out to me and..."

Mia shook her head and he could see her inwardly berating herself.

"It was like my eyes were opened. I don't know that I'd have listened if I hadn't already been having doubts, which scares me. He had these manic highs and lows where everything I did was perfect, but then the next day I was a stupid human who was lucky he was with me. He never said it in those exact words, or I'd have bailed. But I could feel the intent. That he thought I should be grateful to simply be with him, a royal vampire." Another eye roll. "Then there were the lies. Little ones that I'd caught him in. Stupid stuff, but if you lie about little stuff..." She shrugged.

Oh, he hated this Charles with deep, burning dragonfire. Wanted to rip his limbs off and let him bleed out before burning him to ash for treating Mia that way. "Then you lie about the bigger things. If you can't trust someone to be honest with you about inconsequential things, how can you trust them for the real things that matter? How can you trust them with you as a person?"

She nodded again, the tension in her shoulders easing once again. "Yes, exactly. So, I ended things."

Tiber realized he was holding his breath, waiting for her to tell him the fallout of the breakup. Because he could see where this was going. Or at least the direction.

"I was gentle about it, told him that it was me, not him, blah blah blah. I thought he took it well."

"Did he hurt you?" He sounded as if he'd swallowed gravel as he tried to force the words past his throat. If that male had hurt her and was here in this realm now, *Charles* wouldn't live through the night. Inter-realm issues be damned.

"No. Not... exactly. And this is why I think I'm overreacting. I can't *prove* anything. I literally have no proof other than my instinct, which could be completely wrong, that he was behind some weird things in my life. My sister's garden and greenhouse mysteriously burned down. Then I ran into him the next night and he was so strange, specifically asking about her. Then a very close friend of mine was injured in what was supposedly a freak accident at work. But he has no memory of it, just... nightmares. Same deal, I ran into Charles as I was leaving the healer after visiting my friend, and he was off."

"How so?"

"I don't know how to explain it, but it was the way he looked at me. As if he was gleeful that someone in my life had been injured. And maybe that's all it was. But this happened a few more times and he showed up directly after each time someone in my life suffered something. Like a warning. Or maybe he was hoping to see my reaction, to see how much I was emotionally hurt. He asked me out again after the last time and I told him I'd be leaving for another territory. I hadn't even made the decision at that point, but running into him made it for me. I'd just received the invite from Stella—ah, Princess Stella. I didn't say which realm I'd be going to, and made it sound like I'd be gone for years. I've been exchanging letters with my sister and friends, and from all accounts, nothing has happened to anyone I care about since I left. Then... Charles was with the vampire party that night at the auction. And tonight, at the bazaar. I don't know if he saw me."

Oh, Tiber had no doubt the male had seen her, was hunting her. Too bad for Charles, he would never get close enough to Mia again to hurt her. To touch her. The male shouldn't even be breathing the same air as her.

Her cheeks flushed pink as she met his gaze. "I'm sorry how I acted before. I was scared but I shouldn't have used my... I don't know the right word." Her cheeks flushed an even deeper shade of pink and he was certain that yes, she did know the right word. "I should have just asked you to leave, but I panicked. Especially since you offered to cut off his head—and I don't think you were joking. I don't want to make any waves here. I love living here. I moved here when the opportunity presented itself and I would have done it with or without Charles. I don't want to be... a silly human who causes drama."

He frowned at the way she was downplaying things, at the way she wanted to make herself small. "You're not a silly human." His own words ricocheted inside his brain and he wanted to stab himself for his previous thoughtless words. "What you described... you will be staying here at my home until this Charles and his party have left the territory." And Charles would never be allowed to return. He would make sure of that.

"I want to say that it's not necessary."

"And yet it is happening."

"You are the most high-handed person I've ever met." There was absolutely no heat in her voice. "And thank you."

He shrugged. "So you will not argue about this?"

"No. Charles scares me. And you're the scariest person I know, but I trust you. Just... don't cut off his head and cause an inter-realm incident. Okay?" She half-smiled, as if jesting.

But Tiber would absolutely not promise that. As far as he knew vampires turned to ash when they died. He wouldn't even have to hide the body. No cleanup was always a good thing. "Eat your food. You've barely touched it."

She looked down in surprise as if she'd forgotten about the food and picked up some of the cheese. "I can't stay here without Neptune. He'll be fine without me for one night, but I can't leave him longer than that."

"I already thought of that. I'll retrieve him or send someone else to. Do not worry." It was clear how much she loved the fluffy beast.

"Oh... thank you."

As she started to eat, he pulled some more things out and started cooking her a proper meal. But while he worked, he started making plans to end the threat against her for good.

# CHAPTER 10

Mia could feel the warmth on her face and smiled before opening her eyes. Then realized that she was very much not alone in the massive bed (if you could even call it that).

It wasn't the sun warming her, but the reflections from the large gold-amber dragon curled up on the massive hanging bed that was probably the size of a basketball court. Maybe bigger.

Last night Tiber had told her that they could share the bed with him on one side and her on the other or that she could sleep downstairs in one of the rooms. But with a whole basketball court's worth of space in between it was like they weren't even in the same room.

At least that was what she told herself.

But now the giant beast was essentially curled around her. Though he wasn't close to touching her. Even if he was watching her intently. His eyes were the same gold-amber but with more of a mercurial quality.

Blinking, she sat up and looked right back him. "Good morning," she murmured, feeling awkward.

He made a little snuffling sound which she took to mean good morning too.

"You are much bigger than I realized the other day." Aaaand, she wondered if that sounded weird? She didn't mean it in a perverted sort of way, but come on, this beast was huge.

He made another sound that sounded a bit like a purr now.

"Your scales are beautiful."

His head tilted slightly to the side, and she wondered if he could actually understand what she was saying. Maybe she was just reading into things? Oh... she just realized that she had no idea about this! Did shifters in their animal form understand when humans spoke to them? They had to. Right?

"Do you understand me?" she whispered.

He closed his eyes then and leaned back slightly in a way that made it clear he was enjoying the morning sunlight. So maybe he didn't understand.

It reflected off him, bathing her in more of that gold light and she sighed, lying back on the plethora of colorful cushions. "It's just as well that you don't understand. I think your ego is likely too big to begin with to be told you're beautiful." Even if he was beyond stunning.

It almost hurt to look at him.

At a shuffling sound, she opened her eyes again and stared as the dragon disappeared in a puff of smoke, sparks and what she could only call magic.

Then Tiber was crouching about ten feet in front of her.

She squeaked again (seriously, would the embarrassment never stop!) when she saw that he was naked.

And big all over. She closed her eyes and looked away. "Can you cover up please?"

His dark laugh filled the air and she felt more than heard him approach. "I'm clothed."

When she opened her eyes, he was only a couple feet away and was indeed clothed. In what amounted to a loin cloth.

Oh sweet goddess above. It was too early for all these muscles and naked-ness. She was only a mortal, after all. And this... well, he was otherworldly. Might as well confront it. Everything about him was rough and solid, as if he'd been forged from the fire he breathed... and she sounded like an idiot.

See, this was why she painted. She was never going to be a poet.

He held out a hand for her, amusement in his gaze as if he read her mind.

She took it and as he pulled her to her feet, he said, "I can understand you when I'm a dragon." Then, taking her by complete surprise, he scooped her up and jumped off the side of the netting.

Without thinking, she wrapped her arms around his neck and held on tight, willing herself not to squeak again. Seriously, she wasn't a mouse!

"Maybe a little warning next time," she rasped out, resting her fingertips on his chest as he gently set her on her feet. And maybe letting them linger a little longer than necessary. "If there is a next time." Because she wasn't sure she could stay here again. Mostly for her sanity. Especially if he normally strode around without any clothing and oh goddess, she could feel her face heating up at their closeness, at her awareness of how very muscular and basically naked he was. But she knew she wouldn't react this way to just anyone.

Nope, apparently, she was into big, grumpy dragons who didn't like humans.

His gaze fell to her mouth and oh, she didn't think she was mistaking what she saw there. Was he... interested in her? A human?

She frowned, but then he turned away so quickly she could barely catch her breath. Just as well because she needed actual physical distance.

"I have plenty to choose from for breakfast," he said, already striding for the kitchen.

"I'll be out in a minute," she said, heading past the kitchen, but not before he called out.

"No rush. I had some of your stuff couriered over—including Neptune. He's around here somewhere. Take a shower and rest this morning."

She paused in her hurrying down the smooth stone hallway. That had been very thoughtful of him, though she did wonder who had gone through her things and more importantly, who had handled Neptune. Whatever, a shower and some distance sounded wonderful because she knew her cat wouldn't be coming out for another couple hours. It had been the same when they'd settled in the chalet.

She'd used his bathroom the evening before, and it was like something out of a billionaire's secret lair. Or maybe all dragons had stuff like this.

But there was a natural heated spring in one corner with another magical fireplace next to it. She was tempted to get in it, but had no idea how deep it was and the more modern shower was gorgeous too. Lots of pale gold and sparkles in whatever tile or stone had been used in the large bath house. Because this wasn't just a simple shower. The thing had eight showerheads, and she was pretty sure if she set her mind to it, she could use those shower heads for something else altogether than just showering.

"Get your mind out of the gutter," she muttered to herself as she spotted a duffle bag with... toiletries and clothing. Okay, so Tiber was kind of wonderful.

Even if he did think humans were beneath him.

It was so hard to reconcile that first meeting with the Tiber who'd been going out of his way to protect her, to keep her safe.

And she couldn't believe how attracted she was to him. More than anything, that had taken her off guard. She hadn't expected any of this; hadn't expected him to be so protective and to take care of her. It was disconcerting and messing with her head.

The fact that he was built like a god certainly didn't help either.

# CHAPTER 11

Tiber glanced up from the sizzling stovetop as Octavia strode into his place. She wore the typical warrior garb they all preferred, loose pants and a fitted sash around her otherwise loose tunic. Her inky black hair was pulled back in a tight braid and coiled at her neck. Though not visible, she had weapons hidden in her hair and in her sash.

"Why are you here?" he asked, turning back to the stove.

"Well, good morning to you too, grumpy-ass." She made herself at home and went to the cooler to pull out a fruit juice he kept stocked just for her. "I smell the human. Where is she? Or did she already leave?"

"Showering. And her name is Mia," he growled even as he tried not to imagine Mia in any sort of state of undress. He'd done enough of that last night for a lifetime.

He must have shifted in his sleep, something he hadn't done in centuries. But his dragon had taken over, had wanted to protect Mia.

*And she thinks my scales are beautiful, don't forget that,* his inner asshole reminded him.

Tiber ignored him.

"Ah, I know," Octavia said. "I didn't mean anything by it. Apologies.

She's the only human I've ever met."

He just grunted. He knew Octavia didn't mean anything by calling her a human—she felt as bad as he did for insulting humans in front of her. It still shamed him how callously he'd spoken of his future mate's kind.

Even if he'd meant the words at the time. Clearly, he'd been wrong, and he still had to make a proper apology. But the few times he'd tried, Mia had shut him down. And Starlena had reminded him that he didn't have a right to apologize to her if she didn't want to hear it.

As Octavia snatched a piece of bacon from the plate he'd laid them on, he tried to swat her hand, but she was too fast. "To answer your question, I'm here in place of Cyprus. He had something to take care of."

She sat at the island, then turned at the same time Tiber did. He'd heard Mia finish her shower not too long ago and had been wondering when she could venture out. Because he needed to see her, to scent her, to just bask in her presence. Being around her settled something inside him.

This morning, she had on a matching tunic and pants set of a fine dark blue material that flowed around her body as she walked. Unlike warriors who tended to hold their tunics in place with sashes (that also hid weapons and were used for many other things), her tunic fit perfectly, dipping down between her breasts and showing just a hint of cleavage that he shouldn't be noticing.

"Oh, hi." She stopped as she stepped into the galley, gave Octavia a cautious look.

"Mia, this is Octavia. She's one of my people and will be staying here today while I'm gone."

"Oh." She cleared her throat. "I thought this place was safe."

"It is," Octavia said before he could respond. "But Tiber doesn't want to take any chances with your safety. Also, can I say something?" Octavia asked.

Mia looked unsure, but nodded as she stepped a little farther into the kitchen.

"I want to apologize for being an asshole the day we... sort of met. I said some shitty stuff about humans and that's not okay. There's no excuse for it. Just me being a judgy asshole. I'd heard stories about humans and made a stupid judgment based on that. That's it. And I don't think humans are pathetic or anything like that. I was being mean for no reason at all because I wanted to feel superior and that's not okay. And I understand that you don't have to accept my apology or even be okay with me in your space. I know that actions speak louder than words, but I wanted to put it out there. I'm truly sorry." She paused. "And if you'd rather have someone else to keep you company today, we'll find another warrior to hang out."

Mia blinked at Octavia and to Tiber's surprise, gave his friend a soft smile. "That's probably the sincerest apology I've ever heard. And I accept it. I've made assumptions based on nothing other than rumors myself in the past and I'm not proud of them either. So thank you for your apology."

Octavia blinked in surprise, but then grinned. "Okay then. I hope we can get to know each other better."

"Me too." Mia's smile was soft and genuine as she took a seat at the island next to Octavia.

Tiber turned away, trying to hide his expression and... was that annoyance he felt? *He* had tried to apologize to her, but she'd wanted none of it. But Octavia waltzed in here with... a really good fucking apology. Damn her.

*You should be taking notes*, his dragon purred.

After serving Mia breakfast, he nodded at Octavia to walk with him outside. Once they were out in the cool air, he growled. "What the hell was that?"

She blinked at him. "What was what?"

"That... apology." He realized how insane he sounded, but couldn't stop the swell of... what the fuck was that? His chest was tight and he was having that same urge to run his dragon head into the side of a mountain.

She blinked again. Then again. "I don't understand. Are you asking why I apologized? I'm really sorry, dumbass. I hate that I made her feel bad."

He sighed, then closed his eyes for a long moment. "Just ignore me." He opened his eyes again. "Keep her safe and don't allow her to leave my place. I'm still unsure of the level of threat." But he had an idea. Still, he wasn't certain of the age or power level of her ex. He'd passed a background check to get into the territory and that wasn't easy.

"Don't allow her... as in use physical force?" Octavia gave him an unsure look.

"*No*. No physical force. Just convince her that she doesn't want to leave."

Octavia nodded slowly. "What's going on with you?"

"What do you mean?"

"You're being weird. Even for you."

"Even for me?" Tiber's dragon rose up then and he knew his beast was in his eyes.

Octavia raised her palms. "You know what I mean."

"Expand." His voice was gravelly as his dragon pushed at the boundaries, desperate to be free. He should simply stay and keep Mia safe.

To his surprise, Octavia grinned and patted his arm. "Never mind, I think I see what's going on. I'll see you later tonight." Then she turned on her heel and headed back inside the front door.

He wanted to go after her. No, he simply wanted to see Mia one more time. To lean down and inhale her sweet scent and then drag her to the mountains where she'd be safe from any threats.

Maybe this was what Octavia was talking about. He frowned, but headed out instead of giving into the primal urge to kidnap his human.

\*\*\*

"Where's Tiber? Also, are you hungry?" Mia asked as Octavia strode back in.

The dragon female was probably about six feet tall, strong and a little (a lot) terrifying. But in the same way all dragon warriors were. If she really sat down and thought about the fact that the beings who owned this realm could turn into fire-breathing animals, it was humbling. Especially since this one was model-gorgeous, lean and fit, her entire body a deadly weapon, with long black hair that only showed off a face that gods probably wept over. Mia really, *really* wanted to paint her.

"He's working and yes, I'm starving." She started moving around Tiber's kitchen in a way that said she'd been here before and was very familiar with it.

A weird tension settled in Mia's chest. "He just left?" Without saying goodbye? What the heck.

"Yeah, work... stuff."

"I thought spies were supposed to be good at lying," Mia said as she took a bite of whatever the heck this was. It was a mix of a bunch of colorful vegetables sauteed with spices and then topped with some kind of light sauce. Whatever it was, it was delicious.

Octavia barked out a laugh and glanced over her shoulder as she piled the same food onto her plate. But then she added a bowl of fruit and cheese. "I'm an assassin. Not a spy. Big difference." Then she picked up her plate and bowl, her expression contemplative as she moved to sit next to Mia at the island. "And I guess I'm not retired, but I'm not active anymore. Cyprus and I run the current guard—"

"Guard?"

"Ah, like group. The individuals we train are our guard. It's been called that as long as I can remember. I think it's because they're a guard against outside threats."

"Have I met any of them?"

Octavia shrugged. "Probably—though you'll never know it. And you wouldn't have met anyone in our current class, but the active guard, sure. Again, you still wouldn't know them for assassins. They're out and about living their everyday lives blending with their neighbors and sometimes family. Though to be fair, most of us don't have family."

"Oh. I'm sorry."

But Octavia waved it away with her utensil. "Don't be. The guard becomes our family. When I was young, I used to wish I knew who my parents were but..." She shrugged. "If I'd known, maybe I'd never have become who I am now. Maybe I'd never have seen as many realms as I have. I'd never have met Cyprus and Tiber, and I cannot think of a sadder thing. They're the family I choose."

Mia smiled at the intensity of the woman's words. But then that weird sensation was back. "Have you and Cyprus ever, ah... is dated a thing here?"

Octavia snorted. "Hell no. And in case you're curious, I've never screwed Tiber either." Her face twisted up in what was definitely horror.

And Mia hated that she cared. "I didn't ask."

"Uh huh. So what's up with you two?"

"He's... helping me out right now. It's probably nothing, but he's being cautious." Maybe if she said it enough, she'd believe it. "And let's not talk about me. I interrupted you before when I asked about the guard. So you're a retired assassin?"

"Eh, maybe retired is the wrong word. But Cyprus and I run all the new recruits and whenever Starlena or Tiber are out of the realm, we usually run the whole guard. At this point, it's a well-oiled machine, but we're the oldest and..." She shrugged.

"Deadliest?" Mia blurted, because she'd always had a hard time censoring herself.

Octavia grinned. "I didn't want to say it."

"So what does a semi-retired dragon assassin do for fun? Perhaps... pose for paintings?"

Octavia blinked at her. "Is this your weird way of asking me to pose for you?"

Mia grinned, then speared her last bit of food. "Yes."

"I would love to... and maybe you can help me with something?"

"Sure. I mean, within reason." She doubted that Octavia would ask her for tips on killing but still wanted to throw that out there.

Before The Fall in her realm, she wouldn't have been so comfortable talking about killing or assassins or anything in that category. Those words had never been part of her vocabulary or thought process. If anything, she might have judged.

But she'd seen firsthand the warriors, including dragons and other shifters, who'd protected not only New Orleans, but the world. The battles had been savage and bloody and she was so grateful for those who'd fought for virtual strangers, who'd bled for her home and kept her and her family safe. Everything had changed for her after The Fall, and she'd had to sort of recalibrate the way she viewed the world. Or worlds, really. Realms? Hmmm.

"There's this male who works at the castle," Octavia said. "I've seen you and some other artists talking to him..."

# CHAPTER 12

Tiber remained still as he hung suspended using only his hands and feet outside the castle room where the vampires were being housed. He'd remained in human form for this, keeping his camouflage in place as he climbed.

Using various crevices in the stone, he'd scaled the south side of the castle to one of the guest wings where the visiting vampire coven was staying. That had been the easiest piece of information he'd ever received. Spying in one's own territory did have its advantages.

He'd been unable to step onto the balcony because of the spell work he'd sensed cloaking the balcony from outsiders. And if he had to guess, it likely kept the sunlight out, if the open windows were any indication.

The spell work was either from a witch or a powerful vampire, he couldn't tell the difference. He could have busted through it eventually, but that would defeat the whole purpose of spying.

He was here to listen, to gain intel.

*And maybe sharpen your blade on his neck*, his dragon reminded him.

He didn't hate that idea.

So far, he hadn't been able to hear anything of import, just inane conversations about who'd fucked who since they'd been here, who wanted to fuck who, and how much dragons liked to party.

Wind whipped over him as he scaled a couple feet higher. He'd had to strip and call on his natural camouflage before climbing the castle. And if there was one thing he hated, it was climbing naked. Much harder to protect the favorite part of his anatomy without clothing as a buffer.

But it was the only way he could be truly invisible. The vampires inside this wing of the castle might scent him on the wind, but he doubted they'd think much of it since they were in a dragon stronghold.

*Chirp, chirp, chirp.*

Oh no. He turned at the sound of incessant chirping, which was followed by the whoosh-whoosh of dragonling wings.

No, no, no. He hadn't factored this in.

It was Ilmari, who had no doubt scented him on the wind but couldn't see him.

The little one was flapping around this balcony, looking for him. Sweet goddess, he wanted to play. Or more accurately, he was demanding that Tiber show himself and play because Ilmari scented him.

Goddess, he was such a bossy thing—and it was Tiber's own fault. He often took the little dragonling that Starlena had brought back from the human realm with him to work. The baby loved to sit with him and chirp his own orders at the guard, then chirp maniacally as if he thought he was hilarious.

Tiber couldn't shoo him away either, couldn't alert Ilmari to where he was currently holding himself up.

Guilt speared through him at the sad little cries the dragonling made as he swooped up and down, peering onto the large stone balcony. Under the sunlight Ilmari's gray scales took on a silvery hue with the faintest of pale blue lines running through some of his scales.

"Oh my god, look at this little darling." A slender, pale woman with ice blonde hair wearing a long blue dress that covered most of her body stepped onto the balcony. She winced slightly at the sunlight, so he must be right about the spell work.

"Well, hello there." A woman with dark brown skin stepped out next, dressed similarly to the blonde-haired woman. She had corkscrew curls and while the two women looked nothing alike outwardly, he could sense their vampiric nature. Their sameness.

He'd met enough vampires over his lifetime that he could always pick them out of a crowd, and he wasn't certain how he even knew. They were different from other supernaturals. The bloodborns were different, their scents more natural to him. But they were vampires all the same.

"Aren't you just adorable?" the woman with the corkscrews cooed.

Ilmari hovered over their balcony now, chirping away happily to be recognized and adored.

"What is this beast?" A tall man with a human accent he couldn't place stepped out with the two women. "Ghastly thing."

"Oh hush, Charles." The blonde didn't even glance at him, just made kissy faces to Ilmari, telling him how cute he was.

Tiber was surprised at the vampires' effusiveness even as he catalogued that this was Charles.

The vampire who was going to die by his hand. Or fire. Didn't matter.

"You're just jealous he's cuter than you," the blonde said.

"Probably has more game than you too," corkscrew curls said, making the other woman laugh alongside her.

"When you bitches are done mooning over that monstrosity, I'll be ready. I want to check out their library."

Library? That was a much better location to spy than hanging off the side of the castle while the wind tried its best to chuck him off.

He eyed the male as he disappeared inside, finding himself irrationally annoyed by how almost handsome the vampire was. All smooth skin and sleek elegance. More than anything, he was annoyed that the vampire still retained his head.

"We'll be back later, darling," the blonde cooed.

More kisses were thrown Ilmari's way and only once Tiber heard the interior door open and shut, did he reveal himself.

Ilmari chirped wildly and flapped straight at him.

"Brace," he ordered before pushing off the wall and jumping at Ilmari, who caught him, and only wobbled a bit under his weight.

"I wasn't hiding from you. I was working," he said as Ilmari coasted down to the ground.

Tiber called on his camouflage again and Ilmari tried to do the same, but instead ended up shifting the same shade as the dark grayish stone of the castle.

Luckily, this wing was on the back of the castle, so they landed softly on the grass with no audience to see either of them.

"I have more work to do, but go to my home." Though he was cloaked once again, Ilmari had his scent pinpointed and sat perfectly still in front of Tiber. "Home," he repeated.

Ilmari chirped in understanding, then swept his wing out once.

Tiber leaned over and kissed the top of the dragonling's head. "Good boy," he murmured.

Which earned more chirps before the little one took to the skies. He was still a bit wobbly when he flew, but he was much stronger than even a couple months ago.

"Goddess save me," Tiber murmured, grabbing his clothing and tucking it under a rock. He'd come back for it later.

He ducked in through one of the kitchen entrances, mindful not to brush up against anyone. When he was camouflaged, some might scent him, but there were so many scents in the castle that he wasn't worried about it.

The only way he would get caught was if someone bumped into him.

He dodged two castle guards striding down the hallway and taking up all the space by launching himself over them.

For a moment, he thought one of them felt the brush of air, but the two didn't stop for long and continued heading wherever they were going.

Ten minutes later, he found himself in the library with far more people than he'd expected.

This would be trickier than he'd planned, but he'd been in far worse situations.

Even among the fifty-plus patrons, he followed that vampiric scent and found the three from the balcony sitting in a little alcove.

Charles—who was far more handsome than Tiber had imagined now that they were in brighter light—had an old tome in his lap but wasn't reading, just staring into a drink that smelled like... red wine, not blood.

Though Tiber knew the chef had gathered everything their guests might request. Unfortunately, he couldn't simply request the chef poison this asshole. Though poison went against his nature for the most part, he had a whole cabinet of them on hand.

The male looked around, as if sensing him, and it took everything in Tiber not to do exactly what he desired—take off his head in one savage stroke.

This male had hurt Mia, had wanted to cause her more pain simply because he could. The powerful vampire hadn't been able to take that she'd rejected him so he'd lashed out in a way he knew would hurt her. He'd hurt people she loved, knowing that would injure her deeply.

Because despite what Mia said, she wasn't overreacting. She was right to take the threats seriously, to trust her instinct.

"Jesus, Charles, when are you going to stop moping?" corkscrew curls asked without turning around from the shelf of books she was perusing.

"I'm simply sitting here, enjoying the company." His tone was haughty and refined.

Goddess, the way the male spoke reminded him of the fae. Another strike against him.

"You're enjoying nothing except your own misery." This from the blonde. But her tone was gentler as she sat across from him, two books in her hands. "I say this as a friend, but it's time to move on. Your little human most certainly has."

"Yes." Now corkscrew curls sat on the other chair across from him. "And if we'd known she was one of the artists being showcased we'd have talked you out of coming here. You're simply making yourself miserable."

"And it's not like you've even seen her here."

But there was a glint in Charles's eyes that said he had seen her since arriving. That along with something Tiber recognized clearly in his expression, even if the female vampires didn't seem to. Malice.

Protectiveness swelled up inside Tiber as he moved in behind Charles, leaned down close and inhaled his scent. He would never forget the way this male smelled, would never lose him in a hunt.

*Perhaps we kill him right now. Simply rip out his heart and be done with it,* his dragon said oh so helpfully. *We can apologize later.*

As if he hadn't already thought of that.

Charles looked down and away from his friends. "I know I should have told you. But I simply wanted to see her work again, to own a couple of her pieces to remind me of our time together. That is all." His tone was so pathetic, but Tiber wasn't fooled.

This male wanted to hurt Mia. And something told him that if he couldn't have her, he would kill her in the end.

That wasn't happening. The only death would come when Tiber burned this male to ash for daring to come after his mate.

"You should think of her as a bright part of your life and leave it at that. We've all had heartbreak, but if you wallow, you'll spiral..."

Tiber tuned them out as they continued to comfort the male, because despite being camouflaged, he was under the impression that Charles could sense him.

He might not know what he sensed exactly, but his hindbrain knew a threat was nearby. Because Charles's body had gone rigid as he listened to his friends comfort him, and he was subtly looking around.

Too bad for this walking dead man, he would never see Tiber coming.

# CHAPTER 13

"Come in," Juniper called out at Tiber's knock.

He opened the thick door, still camouflaged, saw that Juniper was with her mate, Zephyr. "It's me. Tiber. Didn't want to drop my camouflage without asking for clothes." If it had just been Zephyr he wouldn't have cared, but Juniper was a princess.

And Starlena's granddaughter.

The rules were different.

Zephyr stood, grabbing clothing from a nearby armoire. Unlike Valentina's office, Juniper's was spacious with thick silk drapes over the stained-glass windows, and a plush seating area with snacks and drinks already set out on a gold platter.

It was messier than he would have imagined, with things tossed about, but that wasn't his business. Once he dressed in the simple tunic and pants from Zephyr, he let his camouflage fall.

"Sit, please." Zephyr nodded at the seating in front of Juniper's desk and while the male was all politeness, he would never be a regal prince.

The male had been stuck in a Hell realm for longer than Tiber wanted to think about, every day a bloody fight for survival. There was a wildness that clung to him, was a part of him. Something Tiber understood because that same primal energy flowed through his own blood.

When he'd first been introduced as Juniper's mate, then subsequently been put in charge of a battalion, there'd been grumbling and talk about Zephyr not deserving it. That hadn't lasted long and now he ran a small battalion of three hundred soldiers who specialized in maritime warfare.

Tiber had never personally worked with him, but two of his people had transferred to Zephyr's command and respected him. That was enough for Tiber.

Juniper looked distracted, but she nodded. "Yes, please sit. Is everything okay?"

Tiber didn't want to sit, but since she was royalty, he obliged. "I have some concerns about the visiting party of vampires." He succinctly laid out what he knew and what he'd overheard.

When he was done, both the other dragons were frowning.

Finally, Juniper spoke. "This Charles is from an old royal line. A human and a bloodborn. I cannot eject him from the realm without causing an incident."

Tiber vaguely wondered what kind of incident killing the vampire would cause.

"But I can task some of my people with shadowing them," she said.

"Ah, I have that taken care of." Before he'd scaled the castle wall this morning, he'd already tasked three of his people to shadow the coven in shifts, though right now they were working as a team. He'd seen all of them in the library blending in well, so he knew they were doing their jobs. If they hadn't been, they would answer to him.

Juniper's smile was dry. "Of course, you have. So why are you here? Because I know you're not asking me for permission."

"I'm worried about Mia's family back home. Perhaps not right this second, but I worry this vampire will be a threat to her sister, to anyone who is important to her." It was one of the reasons she'd come to this realm, to try and protect them by removing herself. "And I don't know enough about her family and friends to send people to shadow them." He paused. "Nor do I have a relationship with the Alpha of the New Orleans territory." And Starlena was out of the area so he couldn't ask her for help.

Juniper nodded in understanding. "But I do."

"Exactly."

Juniper looked at her mate and it was as if they had a silent conversation of simply facial expressions. Finally, she turned back to him. "Zephyr and I have been talking about taking a quick trip to see Stella anyway. We can leave tomorrow. I'll speak to King directly once I'm there and we'll come up with a plan for keeping an eye on her loved ones. This won't take care of the problem long term, however."

"I'm not worried about that," he said as he stood.

She narrowed her bi-colored eyes at him. One was gray, the other a bluish-green that reminded him of an ocean he'd visited long ago.

He held up a palm. "I won't kill him in this territory." He paused. "Unless I have to."

Juniper sighed but didn't say anything else.

*It isn't like she can stop us*, his dragon purred.

On that, they were in agreement. He loved his realm, had bled for it, would do just about anything to keep the kingdom safe. But keeping his future mate protected trumped everything else.

And he would neutralize this threat permanently.

# CHAPTER 14

Exhausted and in a bad temper, Tiber finally made it back home. As he approached the illusion over his front door, he scented different individuals. Mia, Octavia and Ilmari.

And someone who had never been here before.

His dragon pushed to the surface, waiting for the order to unleash. Though at this point, Tiber wasn't certain he could control his beast if something had happened to Mia.

Moving on silent feet, he eased his front door open and was greeted by laughter.

Mia's.

Just like that his dragon receded back into slumber even as he soaked in the sound of her joy.

When he stepped into his living area, he froze.

Octavia was standing next to the fireplace in an elegant ballgown similar in style to the one Mia had worn the other night, her long dark hair down around her face and body in soft waves. Normally she wore it in a tight braid and coil so no one could use her hair in battle against her.

"What happened to you?" he demanded, unable to stop staring. She looked so different.

Octavia blinked but he realized his mistake the moment he saw the hurt in her face.

"Oh my god!" Mia exclaimed and before he realized it, she'd launched a projectile at his face.

He didn't bother to swat the soft pillow out of the way since it missed him by two meters.

"She looks stunning," Mia continued.

"I knew this was a mistake," Octavia murmured, already starting to tug at the straps of the dress as if she was about to rip them off.

"No, no, no. Not a mistake," Mia growled as she stalked over to him.

Before he could respond, her handsome friend, the sculptor, stepped out of the kitchen, a drink in one hand, Neptune curled up in his other arm. He simply looked at Tiber and shook his head.

Neptune meowed at Jonothon, then jumped from his arms and skittered away and underneath a pile of pillows.

Tiber briefly wondered where Ilmari was, then figured the dragonling was sleeping up in the net. The young ones tended to sleep a lot when they were growing.

Tiber's dragon flashed in his eyes as a warning to the sculptor—Jonothon—before he looked back at Mia. Then Octavia. "You... look lovely."

Octavia narrowed her eyes at him. "You sound *so* believable."

"You simply looked vastly different than you normally do. That is all. I wasn't insulting you. The dress is... lovely."

"Lovely? Our girl is stunning." Jonothon stepped further into the room, slid his arm around Mia's shoulders as they faced Octavia, who looked massively uncomfortable. "You are going to make tongues fall out of their mouths when everyone sees you. People will offer you the greatest treasure just to bask in your glow."

"You're going to make this guy forget his own name," Mia added.

"Do I look stupid? Tell me now," she growled at Tiber, ignoring the other two.

"No. It was simply a surprise to see you out of your warrior gear, that is all. You look—"

"If you say lovely again, I'll stab you in the thigh."

"Whoever you're trying to get the attention of will be putty in your hands," he finally said. Because yes, he'd been about to say lovely again. "Though if he only pays attention to this version of you, then he is a fool," he added.

Octavia gave him a real smile.

And so did Mia and the male he wanted to punch. They both beamed at him now. Sweet goddess above, he still wasn't certain what he'd walked into but there were clothes everywhere. All over his cushions, some in his kitchen. And what he could only assume were hair products or maybe perfumes given the array of scents filling the air.

"That's so sweet. Sorry for throwing the pillow at you," Mia said.

"Your aim is atrocious."

Mia sighed and turned back to Octavia. "Thank you for such a fun day."

His friend smiled at her. "I should be thanking you. Today has been... enlightening."

Tiber couldn't read Octavia's tone, but she smiled as she started picking up some of the dresses.

"Oh, just leave them. I've still got to figure out what to wear anyway. And I don't want you getting rumpled." Mia waved a hand at Octavia, shooing her away from the mess.

Tiber had to actively stop himself from picking up all the dresses and other things. In all his years of living here, his place had never looked so...

Messy seemed too tame a word.

Chaotic.

Even the nights when his people came over for drinks and mission planning, it never looked like this.

No, his people were of a similar nature to his. Things had homes and belonged there. Not this chaos.

"Someone should clean this place up," he muttered, glaring at Jonothon.

The other dragon shot him a surprised look, then grinned as he flopped down on some of the cushions. "We should have a pre-party here, invite some of the others over before heading to the festivities." His gaze was challenging as he stared at Tiber. "Get really wild."

"Hush." Now Mia threw a pillow at her friend and then stepped toward Tiber, blocking his line of sight from the obnoxious male. "I know we were a bit messy today. I promise to clean up. And I'm sorry I took over your space like this."

He lifted a shoulder, his gaze straying to her mouth. "I don't mind. Are you hungry? Would you like me to prepare you something before we leave?" They still had a few hours before they would need to leave for yet another of the week's festivities. He was already over it but couldn't allow Mia to go alone.

"I'm starving," Jonothon said from behind Mia.

"It's like you want to lose your head." This was from Octavia, currently ignoring Mia and picking up all the dresses.

"You don't need to prepare anything. I can just eat later."

He grunted, not liking that response, and headed to the kitchen. He wanted to tell her what he'd discovered today, but he wasn't certain what she'd told her friend Jonothon. They seemed close, but he also knew the dragon had hooked up with at least two of the visiting vampires.

"So what are you cooking, big guy?" Jonothon sat at the island as Mia helped Octavia in the connected room.

"How about your heart?" He kept his voice pitched low enough that only the male and Octavia could hear him.

To his surprise, the other dragon laughed. "No thanks. So, you want to hear what I know about her ex, or are you going to keep being sulky? Or maybe it's grumpy." He tapped his chin with his finger.

"She told you about him?"

"Just today when I had to hunt her down. So what's the plan? Are we going to destroy this asshole or what?"

He was certain that their ideas of destroying someone were different, but he approved of the attitude. "What is this 'we' you speak of?" He started chopping up vegetables, imagined how good it would feel to use this very blade on Charles.

"I was just messing with you earlier," Jonothon said. "And from what I hear, this Charles is still hung up on Mia."

Tiber simply nodded, hating it. No male could ever walk away from Mia without still wanting her. But this male who had gone after her family, her friends, was a real threat.

"From the little gossip I gleaned, he's here to win her back. Has big plans to offer her gems, a mansion, the works."

"That male doesn't know her," he murmured.

"And you do?"

"Enough to know she won't be won over by shiny things."

"You are not as dumb as you look."

"And you are dumber than you look." He flicked a glance at Jonothon, let the ancient part of him that he rarely unleashed push to the surface, warning him to back off.

Fear flickered in the male's gaze and for an instant Tiber felt like the monster he'd been called before. But just as quickly, Jonothon narrowed his gaze at him. "You wouldn't hurt her friend," he murmured.

"I guess you'll have to wait and find out."

To his surprise, Jonothon grinned. Goddess, the pretty dragon really was dumb. "So what are *you* going to do about this vampire?"

"Nothing you need to concern yourself about." He paused. "But can you keep an ear to the ground with your vampire contacts? Try to learn as much as you can about his age, his power level, anything important related to his lineage." He had the basics from the file Valentina had given him access to, but it was light. Far too light. And there was no way that the vampires had revealed everything about themselves. That simply wasn't done among supernaturals.

He planned to end this vampire problem, but he had never underestimated his opponents. And just because the vampire was a pretty face didn't mean he wasn't dangerous.

"I'll find out everything I can." Jonothon watched with interest as Tiber pulled more food out from the cooler. "Ooh, yum."

As he continued chopping and dicing, he was very aware of Ilmari swooping down from the net above, preparing to sneak attack Jonothon.

Dragonlings at this age were still training their stealth and Tiber had been working with Ilmari to sneak up on others.

Out of the corner of his eye he saw Octavia putting a finger up to her mouth so Mia wouldn't say anything to her friend.

Tiber just kept preparing the food as Ilmari got closer, closer—he chirped loudly the second before he tackled the startled Jonothon.

Mia and Octavia fell back onto the cushions with laughter even as Jonothon sputtered about the "indignity." Tiber turned away so the others wouldn't see his broad smile.

It wouldn't do for Mia to see him laughing at her dumb friend.

# CHAPTER 15

*Dear Robin,*

*I know I'm sending a letter before I've received your newest, but the last few days I feel like I've been living in an alternate reality. Which I think is ironic (probably, I never get that word right) considering I'm living in a different realm.*

*But I stayed the night with that grumpy dragon Tiber. He just wants to keep me safe, I get that. Can you imagine the scandal if something happened to one of the 'weak' humans officially visiting from an allied realm? Do I sound a little bitter? I can't decide if I am. I can't decide anything right now because my emotions are a total mess.*

*Tiber isn't what I expected at all. Also, a baby dragon is visiting him and is the cutest little beast I've ever seen. He reminds me of King's dragon, but a little younger and more mischievous. He pounced on Jonothon today in a sneak attack. Apparently, it's a thing that dragonlings do? I don't know, that's what I've been told. I was also told that he won't attack me. I think the*

*underlying meaning is that I'm a weak human. Okay, I'll stop with that.*
*I'm not bitter, just nursing some hurt.*

*And I know this isn't all about Tiber and his friend talking shit about hu-*
*mans, that it's more about my own issues. Oh, his friend Octavia apologized*
*for what she said, and it turns out she's kind and amazing. I think you two*
*will hit it off when you finally visit. Hint, hint. Come visit me, I miss your*
*face!*

*I realize that this letter has been a ramble of stuff, but that's where my brain*
*is right now. I've got another art thing tonight and I'm worried I'll run into*
*Charles. I think I might make this my last appearance for the week and just*
*skip the others. The anxiety has been churning inside me all day and I can't*
*do two more nights of this.*

*I love you (come visit!),*
*Mia*

# CHAPTER 16

Mia kept her smile in place even though the nerves she'd been fighting all day were at the forefront, ready to take her down.

As in she was pretty sure she might be sick if she got pulled up on the massive stage now occupied by the queen and king of the Nova realm.

Valentina had told Mia that she would be skipped in the introductions because 1) she'd asked to be excluded, and 2) she'd been here for a few months and people already knew who she was.

But so far everyone in her artists' compound had been pulled up and introduced to what felt like the kingdom at large. There were thousands upon thousands here tonight, far more people than she'd imagined. Way too many eyes watching.

Luckily, Tiber and Octavia had created a sort of bubble around her, so no one was too close to their little group. She also spotted Cyprus with some other large (even for dragons) warriors. It was difficult to tell for certain if they were part of Tiber's guard, and she knew he wouldn't tell her. Or she didn't think he would. If they were current assassins, obviously, he wouldn't tell her or anyone else their identity.

But she was curious by nature.

By the time Queen Soleil finished, Mia could finally breathe and practically sagged into Tiber, who'd been a steady sentry behind her ever since
they'd arrived at the outdoor gala. She'd been so worried that there might
be a miscommunication, and she'd end up on stage staring wide eyed at
everyone.

Including her ex. And it would be even worse because she knew he was
out there, watching her. At least now she didn't feel so on display. And
with Tiber beside her, she knew no harm would come to her. That was a lot
hotter than it should be. Mainly because she shouldn't be thinking about
Tiber in those terms at all. He was not for her—even if he did look good
enough to eat in his formal tunic with intricate stitching that no doubt
indicated some sort of service to the kingdom.

Tonight's festivities required formal dress, and instead of street vendors,
there were massive tents held up by some kind of magic in case the weather
changed.

The tents housed a couple dance floors, plenty of tables, and there were
so many servers carrying flutes of something similar to champagne and hors
d'oeuvres (including blueberry cucumber caprese bites she'd been eyeing).

Now that she knew she wasn't going to be called up to face the massive
crowd, she actually wanted to try some of the food. And... she snagged
a drink from a passing tray and maybe drank it too quickly if Tiber's
surprised expression was anything to go by.

"I'm nervous," she said, her tone defensive.

"I didn't say anything." He paused, grabbed another drink, and handed
it to her. "Why are you nervous? I will allow no one to harm you."

Her stomach did a flip at the growly words.

"It's not that..." Maybe it was a little that. She glanced around to make
sure no one could overhear them. She hadn't seen Charles anywhere, and
didn't actually feel him watching her or anything, but her imagination had

always been a wild one.

It was so crowded now, but having Tiber next to her definitely kept people at bay, even as they made their way to the tables to find seating.

"I just don't like crowds. Not like this. And I was worried the queen might accidentally call me up on stage." She wouldn't have been able to say no then. That would have just drawn more attention to herself. "Honestly, I'm just a ball of anxiety on a good day," she blurted, then wished she could take the words back. He was a powerful, confident warrior dragon. No wonder he thought humans were weak and beneath him.

Looking away from him, she took another long drink of the bubbly and made a note to stop after this one.

It was stronger than human alcohol and she didn't want to be carried out of here. Even if the thought of Tiber carrying her spread warmth through her abdomen.

"Here."

She turned to find Tiber holding out his arm toward her.

He nudged his elbow out once in encouragement. "Take my arm and I promise you no one will want to get close to you." He motioned with his other hand. "You can think of this as your anti-anxiety space."

She laughed lightly at his unexpected words. He was definitely different than she'd originally thought. "Thank you." She slid her hand into the crook of his arm, was surprised by how warm he was. The man was pure power and muscle and was going out of his way to take care of her, to ease her nerves. Talk about a powerful aphrodisiac. "You're better than a coat." Something she'd eschewed tonight because it hadn't gone with her mermaid-style shimmery emerald gown that wrapped around her like a second skin and sparkled with every step she took. Jonothon had told her that this dress deserved its day in the sun.

Or night under the moon as it were, the stars and thousands of magical lights blanketing the air above them.

"Sorry if that's a weird thing to say," she added.

"I like that I never know what you're going to say," he murmured. "And for the record, no one holds a candle to you tonight. You're a brilliant gem."

She blinked up at him in surprise, ready to rebuff the compliment, but she was trying to get better about that. To simply take compliments. She knew who she was and had no doubt that she didn't rank in the top anything of gorgeous people here, but his compliment was sincere—and it made it even harder to ignore her attraction to him. "Thank you. Also, where are you taking me, because I'm certain that our table is on the faaaar side of those tents."

"It is, but there's a path we can take that loops around the festivities. Normally it would be longer, but with the amount of people here, it will take far less time, and you won't be faced with the crowd all at once."

"That's very thoughtful." Did that sound like an accusation? Why was he being so wonderful?

He lifted a shoulder. "People from the outer regions are here. That's why it's so crowded tonight. This is considered one of the larger events of the year, let alone this week."

She nodded, then laughed in delight as the stones beneath them lit up under their steps. She was wearing shimmery slippers and they seemed to almost spark under the illumination. "This is beautiful."

"All the pathways around the castle are imbued with the royal family's magic. It's like this all the time."

"Well, it's delightful." She glanced over her shoulder, saw that Cyprus was following them, though he was hanging back a good bit. She wondered where Octavia was and hoped she'd found the courage to talk to the male she was interested in. Mia still wasn't sure what was going on with Octavia other than she "wanted to get someone's attention." "Is there a reason

Cyprus is following us?"

"He doesn't like crowds either."

"That's not fair."

"What isn't?"

"I can't tell if you're lying." She nudged him in the side. "Though I'm pretty sure you are. Because Cyprus seems to get on with everyone. And you have the ability of scenting when I'm less than truthful. Feels a bit unfair."

"Considering the advantage you have, it evens the scales."

Frowning, she started to ask what he meant when Charles stepped out of the trees like a wraith, his movements elegant, liquid, and his presence utterly terrifying.

Tiber tensed next to her, his body going bowstring tight.

She dug her fingers into Tiber's steely forearm, resisting the urge to hide behind him. Because that would just give Charles what he wanted.

"Mia, how lovely to see you. I saw you sneak away and thought I'd catch up. I'm Charles." He looked at Tiber as if he was eyeing a bug. "I take it you're her saveur de la semaine," he practically purred at Tiber.

"This is my friend," she said in a taut voice when Tiber didn't respond one way or another.

He just watched Charles as if he was food.

She wasn't sure if he understood Charles' sad attempt at an insult, but it clearly didn't bother him. If Tiber was her flavor of the week, well, she could do a lot worse.

"It's such a surprise to see you here," he continued, his voice gentle, each word refined, but she could see what she hadn't before. The real man behind the mask. Anger lurked in the depths of his dark eyes, hiding behind his too perfect face and charm that he could drop at a moment's notice.

She nodded politely. "I've been here for months."

"I was surprised the queen didn't call you onstage for introductions." He made a sort of tsking sound as if embarrassed for her. "You are, of course, talented, but there is so much competition in this realm."

Somehow, she kept her smile in place when she wanted to smack his smirk right off.

"Soleil displayed her work in a solo exhibition last fortnight. She would not need to introduce her again. An artist like Mia deserves to shine solo, like the star she is." Tiber's words were perfectly spoken, but she could feel the rage rolling off him.

And she also noted that he called Soleil by her first name. He was making it clear without saying anything what his standing was in this realm. He was also lying through his teeth about a private exhibition, but clearly Charles didn't pick up on that.

His gaze narrowed to slits for just a second before he nodded. "Ah, that is not a surprise at all. I must admit I tried to purchase a couple of your paintings earlier in the week, but they were all scooped up so fast." He said something in French she couldn't understand, then laughed lightly.

She wasn't certain of his exact heritage, but she knew he was from a British royal vampiric line. Yet he spoke French fluently and favored it more than the other languages he spoke.

"I was hoping I could commission a piece before I leave," he continued.

"How long will you be in the Nova realm?" she asked, ignoring the question. She would never paint anything for him.

"Not much longer, I'm afraid. But I would happily return to own something of yours."

The way he said "own" sent a shiver down her spine, but she managed to keep her expression neutral. Hopefully bored, but if she could keep neutral, she considered it a win.

"She has commissions for the next two years," Tiber said before she could respond. "But you're welcome to join the waiting list. If you speak to her agent, she'll be able to help you. Now if you'll excuse us, we don't want to keep our companions waiting." His voice was like liquid gold; deep, delicious and he was absolutely done with Charles. It was so obvious he was dismissing him and even better, Charles knew it too.

She didn't have time to say a word before Tiber basically dragged her off with him.

When she glanced behind them, she didn't see Cyprus or Charles.

"Cyprus is tailing him now," he murmured, his voice so low she almost didn't hear him.

"You were sort of magnificent back there. I never knew how to handle him, even before I ended things. Not well anyway. He always acted like such a baby whenever I told him no, and I realize it's not my responsibility to manage his emotions, but he was so exhausting. And you just..." She smiled. "You just politely cut him off, shut him down, and that was that." When she looked at him, she found Tiber's amber gaze was too bright, too intense, short of shimmering almost gold instead of their normal amber-gold hue.

The way he watched her brought out far too many emotions she didn't want to acknowledge. So she looked away and focused on the glowing stones in front of them as they wound their way back to the party. "Anyway, thank you," she murmured.

"It was my pleasure." There was something else in his voice. Something dark and not altogether human. Or maybe she was reading too much into it, but she swore she could hear the rumble of his beast.

And she liked it far more than she ever could have imagined.

# CHAPTER 17

"You're in a good mood." Nolan sat on the chair next to Tiber, a drink in hand and a scowl on his face.

Tiber glanced at his old friend—who was watching Mia, Octavia and Asa intently. Though Tiber knew the male only had eyes for Octavia and was likely plotting the death of Asa, a kind baker from the castle.

"Why shouldn't I be?" he murmured, his gaze straying back to Mia. Goddess, he loved watching her, and the shimmery dress she was in literally made her shine. Every time she moved, it sparkled with her. Though he'd love to see her out of it more than anything.

Naked, splayed out on his bed, her legs open for him as he tasted her.

Nolan downed his drink, and leaned back in his chair, making it creak under his weight. "Octavia looks different." He frowned harder.

"I hope you were smart enough not to say that." Like he had. "And she looks beautiful."

"Why the fuck are you noticing?"

Tiber shot his old friend a sideways glance.

"What?"

"Just wondering when you're finally going to pull your head out of your ass." He stood, ignoring Nolan's growl of annoyance and made his way over to the trio at the neighboring table.

Mia's friends and his had two tables next to each other upon his request, and it was interesting watching the two groups mingle.

Mia smiled at him as he approached, and once again he had to remind himself to breathe. When she looked at him, bestowed that joy in his direction, he wanted to fall to his knees, shove her dress up and make sure she never stopped smiling.

"Asa was just telling us the secret to making perfect bread pudding."

The male laughed lightly, even that sounding gentle. "It's not a secret, but you use older bread. Still good, but not soft, it will keep the pudding from getting mushy."

Tiber genuinely liked Asa. He'd been with the castle for a couple years, having moved into the territory from one of the outer ones. If this was the male that she was trying to show off for, he was too soft for Octavia. She would run roughshod over the gentle baker. It also wasn't Tiber's place to say anything.

Octavia smiled at Asa. "I'll have to try that sometime."

"Or I can just make it for you." Asa smiled right back at her.

Mia linked her arm in Tiber's and murmured something about needing to talk to him.

"What is it?" he asked as they made their way to one of the drink stations, wondering if she'd spotted her ex or something out of the ordinary. He was on high alert but hadn't seen or scented the vampire since earlier in the woods.

"Oh, nothing. I just wanted to give them some privacy. I can't tell if that's who she's into but thought maybe they wanted to be alone. But I wouldn't say no to another drink—nothing else with alcohol though. The stuff here packs a punch."

He nodded as he plucked up a concoction made with fruits from their coldest territory. "I think you'll like this."

"Oh my god," she practically moaned as she took a sip of the light pink drink. "I've never had anything like this. Sweet but not too sweet and..." She took another sip and made that same soft moan.

And goddess, he wondered what she would sound like when he buried himself inside her.

He gave her a soft smile, but frowned as he realized Nolan had approached Asa and Octavia and was vibrating with too much energy.

Mia leaned in close to Tiber, lowered her voice. "So is that Octavia's best friend? The one I've heard likes her?"

"Ah..." Tiber glanced around, realized a handful of people from surrounding tables were watching him and Mia.

They all looked the other way when he made eye contact with them—and glared. What was going on? Why was everyone watching them?

"Oh, you don't have to answer. I'm just being nosy," she said, leaning in again. Then she swayed into him. Her sweet natural scent made him lightheaded for a moment. Goddess, she was so soft and wonderful. "I think maybe there's alcohol in this? I'm feeling a little lightheaded."

He took the outstretched drink, smelled it, winced at the faintest hint of a locally distilled liquor. It was almost scentless. "You are correct," he murmured, sliding his arm around her, savoring how good she felt pressed up against him. "What would you think if we got out of here? Because I think this is going to hit you stronger than you realize."

"I feel fine, but leaving is probably best. Also, I need to tell you a secret," she whispered as she motioned for him to bend down.

Tension coiled tight in his abdomen as he leaned down... and she gently touched his nose with a "boop."

"I'm sorry, I had to," she said with a light giggle. "You just look so serious. Ooh, you're right, that stuff really is strong." She swayed into him again.

So he slid an arm around her and held her close, making it look like he was simply walking with her instead of supporting her.

She held onto him tightly and only once they were walking among the outlying path around the festivities, did he scoop her up into his arms. The trees gave them enough cover that no one else could see them.

She yelped in surprise but then laughed again as if it was hilarious that he was carrying her and oh yeah, she'd had too much to drink. He resisted the urge to bury his face against her neck and just inhale.

"I didn't think I drank that much," she said as he hurried along the path. He would put her back on her feet as soon as they neared the public area, but he could make good time this way.

"You're smaller than the average intended recipient here."

"Average intended," she said, dropping her voice and giggling some more.

"Is that how I talk?"

"Kinda. So are you and your dragon like separate entities?" she blurted. "Because you told him to shut up the other day."

"We are the same but separate." He had no idea how to explain it, just that it had always been that way.

"Oh, that's much clearer," she said with a snort of laughter. She curled up in his arms, her eyes starting to close and he realized that the drinks were hitting her faster than he'd thought. "You smell good."

His dragon purred softly at that. "I'm going to take a very long way back to my place."

"Hmm."

"Can you open your eyes for a moment?"

"They're open," she murmured, turning her face into his shoulder. "You smell *really* good," she said, inhaling a little deeper.

Oh sweet goddess. "Your eyes are not open," he rasped out, trying not to focus on how right she felt curled up against him, how her scent was making him crazy—how much he wanted her.

"But I can hear you."

He just wanted to see her eyes. "Unless you want people to see me carrying you, then I'm going to take a longer route back to my place."

"I don't care if... okay, the longer route is good. I don't want people talking." She sighed softly, her eyes still closed, and he knew that she was close to falling asleep.

He tried not to care that she didn't want anyone to see him carry her. He'd given her the choice after all, because he'd known how she would feel. Of course, she wouldn't want anyone to see her being carried home after an event.

It wasn't her fault that she hadn't realized how much alcohol she'd been imbibing. And there should be a sign or something for the fruity concoctions. Those things were potent even for some dragons.

Instead of staying on the well-lit path, he ducked into the woods and circled through the forest around the castle grounds. He'd walked this way many times, usually when he wanted to avoid people.

Which was almost always.

He liked his own people, his friends, or chosen family, as Octavia liked to say. But everyone else he could mostly do without.

Only now, he found he cared far too deeply for the sweet human in his arms. While he was physically stronger than her—

*And most dragons*, his beast interjected.

He knew that she had the power to break him in a different way. But she was still physically vulnerable, something that kept him up at night. Among other things.

After meeting her ex, he had no doubt that male wished her harm. It had been in every line of his condescending body language, his tone, and the covetous way he looked at Mia.

Charles hadn't been able to mask that. That vampire wanted her for his own. And the male was deadly, dangerous.

Tiber could easily dispose of him tonight, using the cover of the party, but Juniper wasn't wrong about creating an incident in the territory.

And tricky things like royals getting murdered or going missing could cause great troubles even decades from now. The Nova realm had opened itself up to outsiders, so it was understood that outsiders would be safe here.

He wouldn't do anything to the male unless provoked.

But there was nothing stopping Tiber from killing that vampire once he crossed back into New Orleans. He would tell no one where he was going and wouldn't let anyone see him. He would simply have to make sure  Charles made it home, made contact with some of his people, and once it was established that he was fully gone from the Nova realm, Tiber would make his move.

Though he would prefer to bring the vampire pain, he would make his kill quick and efficient.

He was a master at remaining invisible when he wanted to.

He paused as Ilmari swooped down next to him, the little dragon chirping happily in greeting. His gray wings almost sparkled under the moonlight as he coasted along.

"Hey, buddy."

Ilmari chirped again, then swooped directly over Tiber and leaned down to sniff Mia.

He chirped even louder, his wings flapping faster as he started flying circles around them.

It was clear that Ilmari liked Mia.

"You want to stay at my place tonight?" he murmured.

Ilmari chirped twice, making him smile.

"Okay, use the top entrance." There was an entrance high above his home for any dragons who were welcome, and Ilmari was definitely one of them. "But you have to be quiet tonight because Mia is sleeping. We don't want to wake her."

Ilmari made quiet little chirps in response.

Which made Tiber smile. This dragonling was a lot smarter than others gave him credit for.

As he entered his place, he was once again inundated with her scent, which had now started to settle into his place. Exactly where she belonged.

Even if she didn't realize it yet.

# CHAPTER 18

"Pretty sure we've seen the last of Tiber for the evening." Nolan returned from the drink station and handed one to Octavia.

He'd styled his dark hair tonight, but it was still unruly, some of the curls coming free from his hair tie.

She frowned, but took the drink. She'd seen Mia and Tiber sneak off not too long ago and figured Nolan was right. She was surprised he'd only brought a drink for her, so instead of drinking it, she handed it to Asa with a smile. He really was a nice male, and she hadn't been completely honest with Mia about why she'd wanted to dress up tonight.

It hadn't been for Asa—they were simply friends. A little fib where she'd pretended that she didn't know him well. She was used to lying for work, but she'd actually felt bad using half-truths with her new friend. But for tonight to work, she hadn't wanted to risk Mia snitching on her to Tiber.

And this little "glow up" as one of her friends had called it, was for her dumbass best friend who didn't seem to know she was a female. Nolan only saw her as a warrior. And fine, she was a kickass one, but a woman had needs.

She'd thought dressing up and trying something different would get his attention. But he'd barely said anything about the change and had been surly all night.

Asa nodded at Nolan with a smile because, of course, he did. "Thank you. I see a couple friends I need to talk to if you'll both excuse me." He looked back at Octavia, grinned just a little wickedly. "But save me a dance?"

"Of course. I'll save all of them." Was she laying it on too thick? Whatever, she didn't care. Asa knew what she was up to and fully supported her.

Next to her Nolan growled deep in his throat and once it was just the two of them, he said, "That drink was for you."

"Well, it was pretty rude of you not to get Asa something. And that's not like you. What's going on tonight?" Because her best friend was normally even keeled. On missions she could always trust him to have her back. To have anyone's back. He was levelheaded and the kind of partner you wanted in a shitstorm.

And in your bed.

"He's lucky I didn't smash it in his face."

Octavia blinked, her mouth falling open slightly. "What the hell is wrong with you?"

Nolan shrugged. "I just don't like him. He's shifty."

She blinked again. "Asa. The *baker*? You think he's shifty?" she asked slowly.

"He's not good enough for you, that's for sure." He set his drink down on a passing tray, his jaw set.

And sweet flying dragons, she wanted to punch him. She might trust him with her life, but her heart was a different story. And she was starting to realize that what she felt was one sided. He was just a grumpy asshole who didn't see her as anything other than a friend, a fellow warrior.

Clearly.

She'd thought they had a spark, that things had been shifting between them lately, especially after their last couple missions. But...

She smiled as Cyprus approached, looking smug. Glad to stop obsessing about Nolan, she eyed Cyprus. "You look like you're up to something."

To her surprise, he gave her a little bow, snagged her hand, and tugged her along with him toward the nearest dance floor. "What's going on?" she whispered as he pulled her onto the floor.

This was a familiar song, one of the queen's favorites, and easy to dance to. She preferred her parties rowdier than this, but for a formal occasion at the castle, this was about right.

"You looked like you were ready to set someone on fire, so I figured I'd save him." Cyprus grinned at her as he spun her once.

"I didn't realize I was that transparent." A swirl of color surrounded them as other couples moved on the dance floor.

"You're not—but we've been friends for five hundred years."

"Fair enough." She grinned slightly, letting go of her annoyance at Nolan for now. "So why were you looking so smug earlier?"

"I'll tell you later."

"Ah. Okay." He didn't want to risk anyone overhearing, so it might be official business. As he spun her again, she saw Nolan on the dance floor with one of Mia's artist friends and felt like a dagger had slipped between her ribs.

She turned back to Cyprus. "Feel like getting out of here?"

He nodded and without pause, tugged her through the throng of people.

Goddess, she hated all these stupid emotions she couldn't seem to get a handle on. Some days she wanted to shift to her dragon half and never turn back.

Life was easier as a dragon.

# CHAPTER 19

Tiber opened his eyes to find Neptune about a meter away from him, looking ready to pounce. But then the smoky-colored cat stretched its front paws out and yawned slowly, as if he hadn't been doing anything. After a lazy stretch, the ball of fluff slowly sauntered forward.

"How'd you even get up here?" he murmured.

Tiber had put Mia to bed down in his living room hours ago. He would have put her in one of his guest rooms, but the living room was closer to his bed. In case she woke up in the middle of the night he'd wanted her to be able to use the facilities or kitchen without having to ask him.

Neptune and Ilmari had been down there sleeping next to her, and he would sense a threat in his home, so he hadn't been worried about an outside attack. But somehow this fluffy, hefty cat had made his way up here.

He patted his chest and Neptune moved with liquid grace, jumping up onto his chest with light paws and immediately nudged Tiber's chin with his head.

Laughing lightly, Tiber scratched the top of his head and that little spot right above his tail Neptune seemed to love if the little purring sounds were any indication.

"I'm surprised you're not with Mia," he said after a moment.

If Tiber had the choice, he would be curled up with her right this instant. That was another reason he'd left her sleeping down below. She'd had too much to drink and he hadn't wanted her to feel even more vulnerable when she woke up. It was better for her to wake up with the animals than him.

As if he understood, Neptune meowed, the sound almost indignant.

Frowning, he slowly sat up, giving Neptune time to jump off him. Instead, the cat curled up into his arms, so Tiber held him close as he moved to the edge of the netting.

Ilmari was curled up next to Mia in the array of cushions, one of his gray wings draped over her like a blanket.

"He took your spot, huh?" he whispered. "There's enough room for you too." Moving fast so the cat didn't have time to freak out, he tucked Neptune up against him and tossed down one of the ropes he kept hooked to his bedding. He could have just jumped, but used the rope to slow himself down while Neptune clawed at his shoulders.

When he reached the floor, the smoky-colored cat darted out of his arms and raced for Mia and Ilmari, ducking under the dragonling's protective wing. Then he proceeded to glare at Tiber with big green eyes before he slowly backed away out of sight, his glowing eyes the only thing visible.

*That's the thanks I get.*

Sighing, he headed to his bathroom and straight for the shower. He'd had a few hours of sleep and that was enough for his needs.

And speaking of needs, he desperately had to find relief if he was going to spend another day with Mia in his home.

\*\*\*

At a very loud meowing sound, Mia realized that Neptune was insistently nudging his perfect giant head against her chin.

"Gah, Neptune," she muttered, cracking open her eyes. There was a big blanket over her—nope, that was Ilmari's wing. "I love you, baby, but let me wake up."

*Meow!*

Okay, it was time to get up and feed the big beast. "All right, all right." Groaning, she ducked out from under Ilmari's wing.

He curled into a ball and didn't open his eyes. She looked down at Neptune. "See? He knows what's up."

In response, Neptune wound around her ankles as she made her way to the kitchen. It didn't take long to fill up his food and water bowls and once he was settled, she tiptoed down to the bathroom.

Tiber must still be sleeping and she wanted to get out of this dress—and take advantage of the fireplace and natural spring in his bathroom. She was weirdly glad she was still in her dress and that he hadn't decided to help her get into pajamas.

That was just too embarrassing and the thought made her feel far too vulnerable. She was annoyed at herself for drinking last night, but grateful she didn't have a hangover. Whatever was in those drinks packed a real punch.

Mental note: dragon drinks are not for humans. Especially not her, a lightweight on a good day.

The temperature rose the moment she stepped into the cavernous room and she sighed in appreciation as she stripped off her dress. She gently laid it over one of the bamboo chairs and waded into the blissfully hot water.

He'd told her that it was deep, but as long as she stayed in a certain area, she'd be fine. As she waded down to her waist, she could feel the tension easing out of her body—

She yelped, automatically covering her breasts as Tiber emerged from the other side of the spring.

His amber eyes glittered in surprise and something else as he stared at her. "Good morning." That deep, delicious voice was practically a purr as he waded closer to her, every inch of his wet, muscular torso on display.

Feeling exposed, she ducked down under the water to her neck. "Ah, good morning. I didn't realize you were in here." Clearly. She internally berated herself. Obviously, she didn't know he was in here or she wouldn't have strolled in wearing her birthday suit.

He lifted one of his large shoulders, his eyes firmly on her face. Even so, it was as if he saw all of her.

"It's a large spring, I don't mind sharing. How did you sleep?" Again with that rumble she felt all the way to her core.

"Oh no, I booped you on the nose last night!" The memory popped into her head and now she couldn't unsee it.

He grinned and it turned him from the broody, deadly dragon into something so magnificent she wanted to expire from embarrassment. "You did indeed."

She closed her eyes and ducked her head under the water, wondering if she stayed down long enough if he would disappear.

But nope, when she popped back up, he was leaning against the edge, his arms stretched out on either side of him. Almost as if he was inviting her to come sit in his lap.

Or on his face.

*Oh my god, stop!* she ordered herself. He wasn't inviting anything. She was just overdue for sex. Like *really* overdue. That was it. She hadn't had any physical intimacy in what felt like forever, and she was simply reacting to that.

Not him.

Nope. No, no, no. "I'm sorry about last night."

He shrugged, watching her with that hooded gaze. "You have nothing to be sorry about. If anything, I'm sorry for giving you that last drink."

"It's not like you knew... and thank you for making sure I got back here safely."

"Of course."

She felt awkward hovering under the water so she waded in a little deeper. "Am I good to wade out this far?"

"It drops off closer to that edge." He chin-nodded to the opposite side. "So what are your plans for today?"

She let her head fall back, dipping her hair in the water and enjoying the warmth as she answered. "Meeting with a potential client, then I'm pretty sure I'm skipping this evening's event. I don't have the energy for it after seeing Charles last night. Does that make me a coward?" She raised her head and looked at him.

"No, it does not. You're smart to stay away from him." His expression was dark, edgy.

"I've been thinking about getting away for a couple weeks, at least until he leaves. Part of me wonders if I should go home. I sent my sister a letter, but I don't know if it's enough." She bit her bottom lip, hating that she was so afraid of someone, hating that he was a real threat.

"Juniper and Zephyr leave tomorrow for New Orleans. They're going to speak to King and make sure that your sister and everyone you listed as your references for coming here will be protected."

Surprise punched through her and she waded closer to him. "You asked them to go?"

"Of course."

She wasn't sure how to respond to that at all. "Thank you." She wasn't sure what else to say because that had been so thoughtful. "Tiber, I... just thank you. That's really kind."

He shrugged but didn't respond, just closed his eyes and laid his head back.

So she moved a little closer and realized there was a seating ledge that curled around his side of the spring. "I'm sorry you missed the rest of the party." She sat a few feet down from him, settled against the edge, wishing she was brave enough to test the waters—metaphorically speaking. She couldn't get a read on Tiber, couldn't tell if there might be something between them.

He snorted. "I'm not. I was only there for you."

She'd assumed he would have gone since it was such a big event for the kingdom. Though he'd probably gone to more of them than she wanted to think about. She started to tell him that she was going to make real plans for a little trip and that he wouldn't have to worry about her anymore, when he opened his eyes.

She forgot what she was going to say. Caught in the magnetic power of that amber-gold gaze.

"What time do you meet up with your client?"

"Lunchtime."

He turned toward her and moved down a foot, closing the gap between them even more. And it was like the temperature rose another ten degrees.

"Before you leave for your meeting, I'd like to go over something with you."

"Over something?" She couldn't stop staring at his mouth, the way his throat worked when he spoke. Jesus, was she high? She felt as if she was on something—when she really wanted to get on Tiber.

No. Noooo. He'd made his feelings on humans perfectly clear. Right?

"I'd like to talk about poisons."

Wait... what? Her gaze snapped to his as she digested his words. "Did you just say poisons?"

"Yes. I would like to show you various ways to protect yourself from larger, more physically stronger threats." He paused, as if weighing his words carefully. "Not that I am insinuating that you are weak or—"

"Compared to you or any dragons, I'm physically weaker. As in, I don't stand a chance against one of you." She shrugged, even though she was very aware of how lethal the people she spent time with were. Most of them were her friends and she didn't think about their capabilities in the moment or even in the day-to-day stuff.

But the fact remained, she was still human, mortal in a way that shifters weren't.

Though she wasn't sure why he was bringing up poisons of all things.

He pushed out a breath, looking relieved. "After you've had breakfast and tea, I would like to go over about ten different poisons, their uses and how you can protect yourself against predators. Because you're human and you're smaller than most dragons, they'll never expect you to fight back. This will be your advantage."

She mulled over his words for a long moment. "You just have poisons lying around?"

"Of course not. They're stored properly in a cabinet."

She let out a startled burst of laughter at his serious expression and tone. This dragon was too much.

# CHAPTER 20

*Dear Zia,*

*I hope all is well! I miss seeing you and I'm hoping you and Logan will make a trip to see me soon. I'm sure mated life is treating you well. Thank you again for the snacks you sent from home. And I'm so glad you enjoyed the mating gift. It's such an honor to know that you hung up one of my pieces in your room. I hope you treasure it wherever life takes you. You and Logan are two of my favorite people and I love that you're now mates.*

*And speaking of matings... how did you know that Logan was the one? I know how hard he pursued you (and how hard you made him work for it) and I guess I'm just curious when you knew? If you don't mind me asking? I know this is coming out of left field, but you're a human and he's a bear shifter so I was hoping you wouldn't mind sharing your unique perspective into human and shifter relationships. I'm asking for... reasons.*

*How's the newest job site going? I heard through the grapevine that it's almost done and you're kicking ass as usual. I miss book club and our self-defense classes so fill me in on everything and leave nothing out. Any new matings? Fun gossip? Tell me everything! Miss you!*

*Xo,*
*Mia*

# CHAPTER 21

"Ok so wow, you weren't kidding about the poisons." Mia stared at the array of colorful bottles and blades Tiber had laid out on his kitchen table.

Ilmari was sitting perfectly still, watching them as if he understood what Tiber was doing. Meanwhile, Neptune was sleeping on top of Ilmari's head. The image was seared in her brain, and she'd be painting it later.

"You should paint those two like that," Tiber said as he pulled out another bottle.

She blinked. "I was just thinking that."

As if he heard them, Neptune opened his eyes, turned around in a circle and gave them a view of his butt before he settled back down.

Tiber gave her a look she couldn't define other than smoldery (was that a word?), then turned back to the bottles.

"This first one will paralyze the intended target, but not kill them. The second will make them bleed from their noses, eyes, mouth... everywhere basically. And then they'll die."

She read the labels, nodded, but wondered if she'd remember which was which.

"This one will paralyze someone, but is specifically made for wolf shifters so it packs a stronger punch. There's silver in it as well as other ingredients," he said by way of explanation.

"Oh right, the silver thing." It wasn't a myth as it turned out. The garlic thing with vampires was bullshit, but it turned out that stabbing a vampire in the heart would kill it, and a lot of beings too. Didn't have to be a wooden stake.

"This one was created for vampires specifically." He picked up the pink-colored bottle. "It will paralyze them and eventually kill them. And it has no effect on humans."

"None at all?"

"None. The first three... those will paralyze or kill anything, with different rates of speed."

He indicated the pink bottle again. "This one has something in it that targets the blood cells of vampires. I don't know the chemistry of it, but luckily, I don't need to."

"So what exactly do you want me to do, just carry around poison?"

He paused, watching her closely. "Is that something you would consider?"

"I mean... I don't love it. But Charles also scared me last night." She wrapped her arms around herself and shivered. "I also don't think I'll be able to like... throw this at him or whatever."

Tiber snorted in amusement, his expression so adorable until it returned to the hard, surly male she knew. "You'll be more subtle than that." He moved on to one of the smaller weapons, a knife with an intricately carved blade and handle. Dragons were etched along the handle with incredible detail.

She took it with reverence, running her fingers along the handle. "Whoever did this is a true artist."

"She is a true master—and you might have met her. Hestia of the Domani clan."

Mia's eyes widened slightly. "Yes, of course. I mean, I haven't actually met her, but I know her name. Her stained-glass work is beyond words. She's incredible." She carefully handed the blade back to him.

"I recommend you keep this blade on you at all times. It will be sheathed and secure and will fit in any pocket. I can layer it with poison so it's ready to go at a moment's notice. Because if that male attacks, you won't get a warning and you won't get a second chance."

She shivered again. "I... keep telling myself that I'm overreacting—"

"You're not. Stop doing that to yourself. Your instinct is probably sharper than mine because of the threats you face on a daily basis as a female and a human. That male is a menace. I sensed it upon meeting him. He wants you and he doesn't want anyone else to have you—and he doesn't seem like the type to walk away. He will kill you if he doesn't get what he wants from you."

She soaked in his words, hating that he was right. Hated that her instincts were right, and that she'd ever dated that monster. She should have seen the signs. Ugh. Hearing someone like Tiber validate her fears... "You really sent people to watch over my sister, right?"

He nodded. "Technically, Juniper and Zephyr will be talking to King to set something in motion, but yes. Your sister and friends and family will be protected."

"Thank you again." She'd put Charles mostly out of her mind, had been so glad when all the weird stuff had stopped. She'd figured that he'd lost interest and had moved on. But after seeing him last night, that look in his eyes, she was grateful for Tiber's forethought. "And I'll take the knife." Even though she hated it.

He nodded in approval as he set it down. Then he opened the pink bottle and she watched as he took a brush and painted not only the tip of the blade but farther up as well. "It has a shelf life of about two weeks, then I'll coat it again for you." He paused. "If it's even necessary."

She wanted to ask him what he meant by that, but bit back the question. She could only think of one reason why it wouldn't be necessary—if Charles was dead.

***

"Thank you for coming with me today," Mia said to Octavia. "I mean, I know Tiber ordered you to, but I appreciate it."

"Nah, I volunteered."

"Really?"

"Yep. I like hanging out with you. You're a lot saner than the dragons I work with." Octavia was back in her normal warrior gear today with a fitted tunic, soft-looking leather pants and a couple blades strapped across her back. "And it was interesting sitting in on your meeting."

"Really? I figured you were bored." She'd simply talked to her "agent," aka Xenia. Mia wasn't sure she was her agent in the typical sense, but she ran the gallery where Mia showcased her stuff and handled contracts for her. Something she was incredibly grateful for because Xenia always asked for way more than she would have. She was consistently telling Mia to ask for her worth.

"Yeah, I like watching Xenia work. She's terrifying."

"That feels ironic coming from you."

Octavia laughed. "She's terrifying in a different way. But she's deadly in her own right too. Her older brother trained under me centuries ago and he now runs one of our outer territories. I like her whole family."

"Well, I'm glad you were entertained."

"It was interesting to see how you choose commissions too... So if I wanted to commission something, would I go through Xenia or you?"

"Ah, both. What are you thinking you want?"

"I honestly don't know, but I saw some of the pieces Tiber bought and I can admit, I'm jealous."

"Where did you see them?" Because Mia had been curious where he'd hung them up. She knew from Xenia that he'd picked them up, but they weren't on display at his home.

"Oh, at the training center. He's got one in his office and then another in one of our meeting areas. He's taking great pleasure in showing off your work."

Mia felt her cheeks flush with heat. She didn't think that's what Tiber was doing but didn't respond one way or another. She cleared her throat as they passed one of her favorite cafés. "You hungry?"

"I can always eat," was Octavia's reply.

Which was pretty standard with dragons. "Good. It's my treat since you're giving up your day... and I want to hear all about you and Asa."

To her surprise, Octavia's expression shut down as she opened the door to the café.

"Or not," she said as they stepped inside. "We can just eat sweets and talk about anything else."

Octavia nodded and when they made it to the counter, she ordered the equivalent of what Mia would eat in two weeks. Then when Mia tried to pay, she shook her head. "No way, this is on Tiber."

"Nope. He's not paying for my food."

Octavia simply looked down at her, then back at Isaac, the owner, as he boxed everything up. "Ignore her, it goes on Tiber's tab."

Isaac, owner of The Sweet Spot, winced apologetically. "Sorry, Mia. I'm listening to her."

She pursed her lips together, but picked up the plate with a delicate mini cake that was the equivalent of a Chantilly cake back home. Sweet and fruity and just what she needed today. "You're sneaky," she said as the two of them sat at one of the tables.

Isaac closed soon so there wasn't anyone here but the two of them. And there were only six tables anyway since most of his business was through pop ins and foot traffic. She'd also heard that he catered high-end parties on occasion.

"I'm a dragon, of course, I'm sneaky. But Tiber made it clear that you weren't to pay for anything." Octavia speared a bite of her own cake which was a chocolate concoction topped with gold dragons made of sugar and Mia could only guess what else.

"Wait... like just food?" She eyed the other woman suspiciously.

"Anything."

She took another bite of her cake and mulled that over as she tried not to groan in appreciation. But come on, it was so good. "You're a genius, Isaac!" she called out as he cleaned up behind the counter.

"Still not charging you."

Mia laughed at his dry tone. "I know, but you're still a genius." She looked at Octavia again. "So you're either going to talk about last night or explain this whole 'I don't pay for anything' nonsense. What is going on with Tiber? At first, I assumed he was watching out for me because Starlena ordered him to. And I think that was the reason in the beginning. Now I'm pretty sure he's trying to make up for when I overheard the two of you talking about humans. But paying for everything is over the top, so what gives? I make plenty of money here and I'm more than financially stable. He should know, since he bought some of my pieces."

Octavia shoved more cake into her mouth and shrugged.

"So you're not talking?"

Another shrug, then a grin, but just as quickly the dragon moved into action, standing straight up and smoothly stepping in front of her as the bell over the door jingled.

Mia started to ask her what she was doing, then realized it was Charles stepping through the front door.

Just like that, cold slid down her spine and the delicious treat she'd been eating congealed in her stomach.

"Mia," he said, all politeness as the door shut behind him with a little jingle. He flicked a dismissive gaze at Octavia, then seemed to size her up and smiled politely. "Please introduce me to your friend."

How about no. "Are you following me?" she asked bluntly in a way she wouldn't have in the past. She hated that she'd been feeling relaxed and good then bam, he showed up and ruined everything. Ugh. Why couldn't he simply let her live her life?

"Of course not. I was out for an early evening stroll and saw you through the window. May I join you?"

"We were just about to leave," Octavia said, picking up the bag of treats she'd ordered, still keeping herself between Mia and Charles.

Charles's jaw tightened ever so slightly. But then he pasted on the most polite smile for Octavia. "Would you mind giving us a moment to speak in privacy?"

"No."

Charles blinked at Octavia's blunt response.

Even Mia did a double take as she smothered a smile. "You can speak in front of her," Mia said as she got to her feet. "But she is correct, we were just leaving. I've got a few more stops to make this evening."

"I must confess I wasn't following you, but I did seek you out. I wanted to apologize for my behavior when we broke up."

There was no we—she broke up with him—but she didn't correct him.

"I acted poorly, but in my defense, I've never felt that way about anyone before. Not in the hundreds of years I've been alive."

Oh barf, had he been this transparent before and she just hadn't seen it? She cleared her throat. "Thank you for your apology. I accept it and would like to simply move on. I hope you enjoy the rest of your stay in the realm." She started to leave when he took a step forward.

"Have dinner with me? So we can talk? Tomorrow evening. You can meet me at the castle."

She wanted to say no, but there was a glint in his eyes that had her feeling uneasy. Even as she ran her fingers over the handle of her sheathed weapon, she nodded and lied through her teeth. "Ah, sure. Tomorrow sounds good. Now we really must go."

Octavia stayed in front of her, basically shooing him back as she opened the door for Mia. Only once they were alone out in the cold, fresh air, could she breathe again.

"You're not going out with that male," Octavia growled in indignation when they were about two blocks away.

Mia shot her a glance. "No, I'm not. But not because you're telling me what to do. I'd never planned to go out with him. I'm going to send a message to the castle canceling as soon as I get back to Tiber's."

"You should have just said no to him. It sends a stronger message."

"I don't need anyone telling me what I should or shouldn't do," she snapped with more force than she'd meant to. "And you don't have the same lived experiences as me. I said yes now because I was worried how he'd react if I said no. He would have either pushed and pushed until he made a scene or he might have done something worse. I have no way of knowing what his reaction would be, so getting out of there was my main priority. You're not a human so you can't understand what it's like to be physically weaker. I have to make decisions like that every day. Not as much here, but back home? Yeah. I had to make calculated decisions based on how I think those stronger than me will react." And she still did it here too, mostly subconsciously.

"Wow."

"What?"

"You're right. And I'm sorry for being pushy. Also... I can see what Tiber sees in you," she said with a grin. "Feisty little thing."

"Little?"

"Is short better?"

"Oh my god," Mia said with a laugh. "Neither one! But feisty or sassy are fine descriptions."

"Noted. And I'm sorry you have to make decisions like that."

"Me too... If I write a letter to him, will you drop it off at the castle for me?"

"Of course."

"Thank you... I might have another note for you to drop off if you don't mind. I know this isn't your job."

"I'm doing it as your friend, and, of course, I don't mind."

Relief swelled inside her. "Okay, well, thank you again."

"After I post the letters, what would you think if I invited some people over to Tiber's place?"

"He won't mind?"

Octavia shook her head. "Nah, he's dealing with some stuff, won't be back until later."

It would have been nice if he'd told her, but Mia guessed it didn't really matter. "Is this like a party or something else?"

"It's games and food. And trash talk."

"That sounds better than a party." Because she was skipping the formal meet-and-greet tonight and the party tomorrow. And if she received the response to her second note that she was hoping for, she'd be leaving soon for one of the outer territories for a bit.

Was she running away from Charles to keep things from escalating and prevent him from targeting anyone else she cared about?

Absolutely.

And she was also running away from her feelings for a grumpy dragon who would never see her as a worthy mate.

# CHAPTER 22

Tiber stepped into his home to pure chaos. Or maybe not chaos, but noise, laughter, and an overwhelming amount of food.

Four of his warriors, Mia, and Octavia—as well as Ilmari and Neptune, who was sitting in Mia's lap—were sitting around a table someone had set up right next to his fireplace and playing a board game.

"I think you are scamming us," Angel muttered good-naturedly. "There's no way this is your first time playing."

"Why can't it be my first time playing?" Mia asked tartly, looking at Angel.

"Because..."

"Yeah, keeping your mouth shut is the best idea you ever had," Octavia said with a laugh when Angel couldn't respond.

"There's a similar game back home I've played before," she said as she rolled the dice. "And I always dominate!"

"Savage," Angel murmured, with Baisas groaning.

"You just captured my castle," Baisas said.

"*Four* of your castles," Mia corrected, then grinned when she saw Tiber. "Hey, when did you get back?"

The others had definitely been aware of him, but his human didn't have the same sensory abilities and he'd been enjoying just watching her. "Just walked in. I see you're destroying my people."

"You better believe it." She stretched and stood as Octavia took her turn. "Your friends swore you wouldn't mind them throwing a get together here," she whispered as they reached the kitchen. "Also, they brought fresh bread and so much food." She smiled as she said it, her gaze straying to what was left of the loaf of seeded bread.

"They're always welcome here. I hope tonight wasn't too overwhelming."

"No, I love stuff like this. At the artist's enclave we have game nights or book nights or whatever at least three times a week. I just don't like big crowds." She started making a plate for herself, then looked up. "Are you hungry?"

He was a little surprised by her good mood considering the message he'd received from Octavia but nodded. "I could eat."

She snickered and grabbed another plate, started piling it high with meat and cheese.

It was foreign to have another person making him a plate, but... he liked it as much as he liked cooking for her. But then he frowned when he saw her bags in the corner by one of the windows. "Why is all your stuff packed?"

"That's what I was going to tell you. Octavia and I had a run-in with Charles," she said as she slid him the full plate. "I'm tired of worrying about him and it's not fair that you have to keep housing me so I'm going to take a break and head into the mountains for the next month."

He was very aware of the others in the room quieting down and listening to them while not appearing to try to eavesdrop. And they were no doubt aware that he wanted to keep her here. "Housing" her wasn't an issue.

He would give her his place if she asked. Preferably with her sharing a bed with him. His people knew it, but she, clearly did not. "Why the mountains?"

"A friend of mine is staying up there because she wanted a new setting to work and said I have a standing invitation. I've been thinking of going and figured that now is the time. Though I do appreciate all you've done. I hope... that you think of me as a friend now. Even if I'm just a silly human," she added, her grin mischievous.

"I'm sorry for what I said. Officially," he added. "And you're going to listen to my apology." And, apparently, all his warriors were getting to overhear as well. "Because I mean it. You are not a silly human, and I don't want you to feel like you have to leave. I will handle the issue with Charles tonight. I'm going to head to the castle and talk to the queen directly. She'll make an excuse for kicking out his whole party and make it sound like it was their idea."

But Mia shook her head and moved around the island, gently touching his forearm. "No. I mean, I appreciate it but no. I don't want any issues with his coven. And thank you for the apology. I accept it and I meant what I said, I hope we can be friends... what's wrong with you two?" She stared as Octavia and Angel basically stumbled into the kitchen, both clutching their chests.

"The great Tiber has apologized," Octavia bemoaned, clutching her chest theatrically.

Angel fell to the floor, spreading out on his back as Neptune jumped on his chest, staring down at Angel curiously. "The world must be ending. It is the only explanation for this apology."

Tiber looked at Mia. "This is why I don't invite these assholes over very often."

But she giggled and threw a cheese cube at Angel. "You're ridiculous."

Octavia snatched a hand out and caught the cheese. "I don't think you understand what a big deal it is for Tiber to..." she lowered her voice, whispering, "apologize."

"Assholes. Every single one of you." But he found himself grinning, especially when Neptune turned around and tried to put his butt on Angel's face. Tiber really did like that cat.

"Hey! I thought we were cool, Neptune," he sputtered, jumping to his feet.

Tiber crouched down and fed Neptune a bit of turkey. "Good boy."

"He really likes you," Mia murmured as he scooped Neptune up in his arms, the little guy purring.

That was when Tiber realized that she was watching him with an expression he wasn't sure he could read.

He wasn't sure what to make of it, but what he did know was that she wasn't going into the mountains by herself tomorrow. He'd be escorting her and then he'd be making her his mate.

He'd never thought to fall for a human—or anyone, if he was being honest with himself—but she was part of the fabric of his life now. That was it. He wasn't letting her go.

# CHAPTER 23

*Dear Aurora,*

*I can't thank you enough for introducing me to Stella and 'suggesting' that I visit the Nova realm. (Are you ever going to get sick of me thanking you? Too bad, you changed my life and I'm always going to be grateful!). It's been a wild ride and tomorrow I'm off on another adventure out into a mountainous region here.*

*I miss your classes and guidance, and just getting to see you so much. But I've heard such positive things about New Orleans (as if there would be anything else) and love how much you and King are doing for the territory. New Orleans will always be my home, but I think I might call Nova home for a while too.*

*I've also recently been introduced to one of the dragonlings who came from New Orleans and he's just as silly as Hunter. I wonder if he and Ilmari are brothers? Either way, he loves Neptune and seems to have the same affinity for felines as Hunter. Or maybe not as much as Hunter since last I heard, he's amassing a cat army all by himself. But I wanted to tell you that the dragonlings here are thriving and happy.*

*Just like me. I hope you're doing well and look forward to your next letter.*

*Xo,*
*Mia*

*P.S. Remember Tiber, that rude dragon I told you about? Turns out he's not terrible at all. He's kind of wonderful (and protective) and has been letting me stay with him. After tomorrow I won't see him for a while, but I wanted to set the record straight since I'd mentioned him before. We got off on the wrong foot, but things are good now. Love you!*

# CHAPTER 24

Feeling refreshed, if a bit nervous, Mia stepped into the kitchen as she finished braiding her damp hair—and froze.

"Why do you have bags next to mine?" she asked Tiber, who was casually drinking tea.

"I made you tea," he said in response, nodding at the fresh pot on the stove. "And I'm going with you."

"Wait...what?" Last night she'd told him that she was heading out this morning and he'd been fine with it. Had even joined her and the others in a board game. She'd beat him too. They really needed to learn better strategy when it came to building cities.

"I'll be going with you. You have no experience traversing our mountainous terrain and it's not for the faint of heart."

"First of all, I hired someone. So I'm good. I guess there's no second of all." Clearly, she needed some strong tea this morning. "And I know you can't spare the time to travel. And before you say anything, Octavia recommended a guide so it's not like I just hired some random person. This man is trained, and I've already paid him. So you can rest easy and let Starlena or the queen or whoever know that I'm safe and will be out of pocket for about a month. I've already let Xenia know and she's happy," she added. "She's hoping I'll come back with even more inspiration."

"I let your guide know that his services aren't necessary." Each word out of his mouth was clipped. "And he's reimbursed you. I paid him what you would have owed him so he has no hard feelings either."

"Tiber!" She wanted to stomp her foot even though it was a childish impulse. "You can't just... do that."

"But I did." He took another sip, looking almost smug. And fine, he was painfully gorgeous as he stood there sipping tea.

"Tiber."

Now he smiled.

"Oh my god, you're driving me crazy."

"Why? I'm an excellent guide, an excellent tracker and I will get you to your destination much faster than that... guide." The way he said guide sounded as if he was saying "pile of crap."

"Octavia said he was the best, very skilled."

Tiber shrugged again. "I'm better."

She covered her face with her hands. "What is going on with you? Your duty is over! You don't have to keep me safe anymore. I'm very appreciative of all that you've done. Seriously, you've gone above and beyond. And I've accepted your apology. More than your words, you've shown me who you are. But you don't have to do like... whatever this is. Some weird version of penance. I promise, you and I are good. You owe me nothing." And she needed some distance from the distracting dragon.

"Would you like breakfast before we leave?"

"Am I a ghost? Am I talking and you're just not hearing?"

"You would make a beautiful ghost, but I can hear you just fine. I'm choosing to ignore you because I don't wish to argue with you. I'm going with you and that's that."

Her heart stuttered for a moment and she tried not to get hung up on the "beautiful" comment. "What about your job? I know what you do for the castle is important."

"Plenty of people can take over for me. I'm just a cog in the machine."

"Lies!"

He shrugged. "Octavia and Cyprus will be taking over."

She let her head fall back and stared up at the ceiling, realized Ilmari was watching her from the netting above. "Are you coming too?"

He chirped in what sounded a whole lot like a positive response.

Sighing, she looked back at Tiber. "I'd like to make it clear that this..." She motioned at him. "This not listening to me, is not okay. I'm not okay with it."

"When it comes to your safety, I'm not bending. I'll bend on almost anything if you ask, but not this. You will stay safe. And I'm not leaving your safety in the hands of some guide—or anyone else." There was a finality to his words that sent a shiver down her spine. But unlike the iciness she experienced around Charles, this was wholly different.

Also, it was really hard to get mad when he wanted to keep her safe. But for her sanity she'd been hoping for distance from him. Especially after the evening last night with him and all his warriors. He'd been so relaxed, and she'd been able to see the other side to Tiber.

The kind male who'd been looking out for her ever since the gallery auction.

"I already made you breakfast," he finally said, breaking through the silence. "Your favorite."

He'd been cooking her something similar to Migas from back home and... apparently, she was weak. "Thank you. For breakfast and for caring. I just hate that you're taking time away from work. I was being serious before, I know how important you are to the castle." Or she could guess considering the deference so many others gave him.

"They have survived without me and they will again. Now sit, eat. Are we bringing Neptune?"

"Ah, no. Jonothon is going to pick him up this morning. He's a good traveler, but I worried it might be too rough for him. And Jonothon and him are two peas in a pod."

Tiber simply grunted at the mention of Jonothon, but nodded.

And apparently, that was that. He was coming with her.

She wasn't sure how she felt about it. *Liar, liar.* She was simultaneously excited and worried. She was starting to catch feelings for the big dragon. Or more accurately, she'd caught feelings for him.

And while he might be apologetic for what he'd said, and he'd gone out of his way to keep her safe, she still didn't think he would view her as a potential... whatever. Lover? That was sort of a gross word. Girlfriend? Also weird.

A hookup?

Ugh, she didn't like that either.

And she shouldn't even be thinking about that anyway. They were just... friends? Yeah, she was pretty sure they were friends at this point.

Even if he was over-the-top bossy.

# CHAPTER 25

Mia wondered why they were landing until Ilmari burst through the thicket of trees after the much larger Tiber and saw the gorgeous hot spring surrounded by a haven of green. Even with it being so cold, the trees and plants surrounding it were lush and thick. A small waterfall added to the picturesque slice of perfection.

She slid off Ilmari and turned around to give Tiber privacy to change into clothing but then she heard a splash and looked back to find him backstroking through the water.

And sweet flying dragons... She turned around so she wouldn't get caught staring.

"Come on in, the water feels great," he called out.

Ilmari trotted away, then took to the air, likely to hunt for food if she had to guess.

"Turn around and I'll get in," she finally said.

The air was already warmer in this little oasis, a stark difference from how chilled she'd been up in the air.

"I'm turning."

She checked to make sure, then stripped down to nothing, piled her hair on top of her head and hurried into the water. She yelped at the rush of heat, but savored it as she dug her toes into the silty bottom. "Don't turn around," she said even though he hadn't given any indication he would.

Nope, he still had his very broad, muscular back to her and oh... he had a lot of scars. Nicks and what had to have been deep gouges at one point to remain as scars. She knew how fast supernaturals healed so... She realized she was close enough to touch him—and had been planning to run her finger over one of his scars.

Maybe he needed to tell *her* to turn around at this point.

"I'm right behind you," she said. "Just letting you know so I don't startle you."

He let out a bark of laughter and turned. "I heard you coming, but thank you for the warning." His gaze flicked down for a fraction of a moment to where she was holding her arm over her breasts.

The water here was much clearer than the spring in his bathroom and she was very aware of just how much he could see considering how bright the sun still was. He had no self-consciousness about anyone seeing him naked. But she did. "Were you getting tired?" she asked. "Not that I mind, it's nice to have a break."

"Not me, but I thought Ilmari might. He's still young to make a trip like this." He paused. "And I figured you could use one too. Besides, this spring is good luck."

She ducked a little lower in the shallow water even though he was still at waist level. He might be okay with all this nudity, but she didn't think she'd ever be so blasé about it. As an artist she loved the human form and had no problem painting nudity but... nope, she was never going to be okay just strutting around in the buff.

She used the mention of Ilmari to turn around and feign looking for him. "You think he'll be okay?"

"Of course, he's just gone hunting."

Sighing in pleasure, she ducked down all the way to her neck. "This place is amazing. I can't believe it even exists. I didn't even see it from the air."

"It's a little secret for those in the know." He grinned, much more relaxed than he'd been back at his place this morning. His amber-gold gaze sparkled in the sunlight, his dark hair slicked back and a little longer than normal now that it was wet. It hit the bottom of his ears and she found herself wondering what it would be like to run her fingers through his thick hair while... well, while they did a lot of things.

She'd been so frustrated with him for insisting on coming with her but now that they were here, she was glad he was the one taking her and not a random guide. "So are there any animals in here I should worry about?" Mia looked around the clear blue-green waters and didn't see anything.

"Oh yeah, but they'll keep their distance since I'm in here."

"What?" She moved closer to him, the water splashing around her. "Are they like biting... You're messing with me!"

When he just laughed, she splashed him—and he laughed even harder.

"You're so easy."

She found herself laughing with him, surprised at this change in him. He was so... relaxed. So different than the sort of scary general back in Nova. She thought about commenting on it but decided against it because she didn't want to ruin the moment of whatever this was.

At the sound of a large rustling from the trees, she froze.

Tiber quickly swam to the edge and then walked out in the direction of the noises. Too afraid to turn away in case it was some random beast come to attack, she stared after him (and tried not to focus on his gorgeous ass).

"It's fine, just Ilmari," Tiber called out from behind the trees moments later. "I'm going to help him clean his hunt."

"Okay," she called out, then fell back into the water. Disappointment slid through her that she'd be alone, but she eventually stretched out on her back, enjoying the feel of the sun bathing her in even more warmth. She hadn't planned to get her hair wet but didn't care at this point.

Combined with the water, this was better than a spa day or a beach day.

She wasn't sure how long she floated in the water, but when a shadow fell over her, she opened her eyes.

And found Tiber staring down the length of her body, heat in his gaze.

But just as quickly he turned away.

She scrambled to her feet, covering her breasts as she stood in the waist-high water, though he was fully facing away from her.

"I called your name but you must not have heard me," he rasped out, every line in his back pulled taut.

She imagined what it would be like to have the right to touch him, to caress him, to trace all the hard lines and striations of not just his back, but everywhere.

The waterfall rumbled close by, likely the reason why she hadn't heard him. "Ah, sorry."

"I just wanted to let you know if you want to eat, drink and take care of anything else, I'd like to leave in the next ten minutes. I want to make sure we make it to our camp by dark."

"I'll get dried off and eat a little," she said, wondering what he would do if she moved in behind him, wrapped her arms around him—pressed her breasts against his back. Reject her? Or turn around and take over?

A small ache pulsed between her legs at the mere thought of what he might do and she tried her best to shut it down. They had a few more hours of travel and despite a few heated looks from him she wasn't under any illusion that they were in the same league.

He was a warrior dragon revered in this realm and even though she was a guest of the queen, she knew her place. She was just a human visiting for now.

# CHAPTER 26

Tiber stripped off his tunic and hung it up on the boulder he was using to protect Mia and their campfire from the winds. Then he stepped around to the other side to find Mia sitting by the fire bundled up in a thick coat, a cap covering her hair and ears. They'd made it here just under an hour ago and he was glad because she had been getting cold in the air.

But she smiled when she saw him, lifted her mug of tea. "I was wondering if you'd forgotten about me."

Impossible—he could never forget her. Especially after seeing her floating naked out in the spring so free and... goddess. She'd been glorious, her hair floating around her, her breasts full and begging for his touch. But he half-smiled at her joke as he approached. "I was helping Ilmari chase down his latest prey. He's still a young hunter, doesn't quite understand the delicacy of the hunt."

"So he's not a vegetarian like some of his siblings back in New Orleans?"

Tiber blinked. "Absolutely not."

She chuckled and stretched her legs out in front of the fire. "I can't believe we've been traveling all day. I've taken mental pictures of everything we've seen, and I want to paint all of it." There was wonder in her voice and he tried to see things from her perspective.

He'd been flying these mountains and this region for centuries but there was no denying the raw beauty of their surroundings. "I hope to purchase some of those paintings."

She shook her head. "No, I'll paint you something for free. For being such a good tour guide and giving me this gift of travel."

He wasn't sure how to respond as he crouched down next to her, enjoying being in her presence as well as the warmth of the fire. He didn't want to be her tour guide. He wanted to be her mate, and his dragon was prowling right at the surface.

"You're not cold?" she asked, her teeth chattering.

He shook his head and stoked the fire even higher. He thought of breathing some of his dragon fire onto it but wasn't sure how she would react. He also seriously contemplated just pulling her into his lap to warm her up but didn't think that would go over well. "Did you get enough to eat?" He'd brought dried fruit snacks and other easy to eat food full of protein, as well as the tea she liked.

Unlike her, he simply hunted for his food in dragon form and ate what he needed. But she was human, and he found himself planning ahead for her needs. Something he'd never had to do before—but he enjoyed taking care of her.

"Yes, thank you. And thank you for the tea. I feel a bit useless since you set everything up." White wisps of vapor curled in front of her as she spoke.

He shrugged, once again resisting the urge to pull her into his arms and keep her warm in a much different way. "There's no sense in both of us doing it when I've done it a hundred times."

"Really?"

He lifted his shoulder again. "I've taken this flight path many times before. Not to your artist's retreat, but other territories."

She made a *hmming* sound and looked back at the fire and he wished he knew what she was thinking.

After seeing her floating gloriously naked in the secret hot springs he'd never shown to anyone else, he couldn't get the vision of her out of his mind.

Didn't want to.

But he also couldn't concentrate now that he knew exactly what her perfect pink nipples looked like. She'd been stretched out like an offering and now he was obsessed with the thought of pleasuring her, making her climax against his mouth, around his cock.

To be fair, he'd already been obsessed with it, but it was worse now.

"Where's Ilmari?" she asked into the quiet, looking up at the dark skies.

Clouds had moved in, hiding the blanket of stars and moon. This high up on one of the mountainsides, they were likely to get fog as well.

"Enjoying his food," he said dryly.

She giggled lightly. "He is a bit of a messy eater."

"If you don't mind, I'm going to get some sleep now. I want to be rested for tomorrow's flight."

"Oh, of course. I'm tired too—and I know you must be a million times more exhausted since you flew all day."

"It wasn't bad." And he'd enjoyed flying next to her and Ilmari. Normally the thought of slowing down for someone else would have annoyed him, but, apparently, nothing about Mia bothered him. He wished she'd asked to ride on him, but he hadn't wanted to pressure her when she was already stressed about her ex.

She crouched down on her bedroll next to his, frowned at the space between them, then to his surprise, she moved her stuff closer.

He hadn't wanted to crowd her, so he'd been cautious. He was well aware of the physical power dynamics and never wanted to make her feel intimidated. "I can sleep in my dragon form and you can curl up under the protection of my tail and wings," he said as he unzipped the roll. "If it'll make you feel safer."

"I think I'd rather you stay in human form—only so we can talk a little. I'm not insulting your dragon half."

*Of course she's not, we are perfect*, his dragon purred. *But I do like the acknowledgement.*

Nodding, he started to unroll his bedding and realized there was a piece of parchment tucked under his pillow.

"Oh, it's nothing," she said hurriedly. "When you were gone, I decided to sketch you and Ilmari. I thought you might like it." Her tone was a little higher than normal, as if she was embarrassed. "You don't have to keep it."

"It's beautiful, I love it. Thank you." He smiled at the black and white drawing of what was clearly him and Ilmari in flight, the much smaller dragon swooping around his left wing in play.

Carefully, he tucked it in one of his leather journals so it would stay flat and protected, then put it back in his satchel.

As he started to get into his bedding, he realized how far they were from the fire. And that it wasn't going to work for her the whole night.

"Hold up," he murmured before he quickly moved her bedding closer to the fire, then his own behind hers. "I'll sleep behind you and keep you warm as well."

He couldn't tell because of the shadows but her cheeks seemed to pinken as she nodded.

Only once she was in her bedroll, did he slide in next to her. Instead of pulling her close, like his dragon demanded, he tucked one hand under his head and half turned toward her. "Did you still want to talk?" he asked quietly. He would talk all night if she wanted, though he had no idea what to say.

She slid one hand under her cheek and turned to him, her coat hood pulled up over her head. Goddess, she was adorable and gorgeous at the same time. "Only if you want to."

At his nod, she gave him a soft smile.

"Will you tell me about where you came from? I've heard enough talk that you're from a desert region?"

He nodded and scooted a little closer, enjoying the way her orange blossom scent carried on the air, seemed to wrap around him.

"My clan was small..." He searched for the right words and then decided not to downplay where he came from. "We were not a peaceful clan. I don't think we're built that way. We often found ourselves at war with other clans."

"Did you enjoy it?"

He paused as he thought about the answer. "I... don't know. It's all I've ever known. I liked fighting alongside my siblings."

"Siblings?"

"A brother and a sister. Both living in different realms. We were always nomads, I guess you could say. My original clan, the ones who remain in my homeland still call the desert their home. They live in gorgeous caves, their lives different than mine. For the most part, they stay in their dragon form. They only shift to human when they need to trade."

Her eyes widened slightly at that. "Do you miss your homeland?"

"Yes and no." He'd never opened up to anyone about this, but he liked telling her more about himself. And he wanted the same from her, to know all her secrets. "I miss my family and carry my childhood memories deep in my heart, but... I love the Nova realm. It's my home in a way no other place ever has been. Octavia likes to say I found my family here and she's not wrong. Nova is my home."

"I love that. Found family." Her eyes grew a little dreamy as she watched him. "You're different than I originally thought."

"Different?"

She bit her bottom lip and goddess, he wanted to take over, to pull her onto him and ravish her mouth. "I'm not sure if I should say."

"You can say anything to me."

"You have a fearsome reputation. One I have no doubt is earned. But... I don't know." She let out a little laugh. "Just ignore me. I'm enjoying hearing about how you grew up. Do you ever visit your family?"

"Occasionally. And my parents have both visited Nova."

"What did they think of it?"

His mouth curved up. "That it is too civilized and its people too soft."

"Soft?"

He snorted. "Yes. Soft. No matter that it is one of the strongest dragon holds," he said, shaking his head. "It's simply different than what they're used to. There's more structure, more... life. I might not enjoy being around others all the time, but I like the pulse of Nova. I feel the rhythm of it in my bones every day."

"That's beautiful," she whispered, her gaze falling to his mouth for a moment.

He wondered what she would do if he reached out, grasped her hip, and made his intention clear. Would she reject him? It was too soon to tell, and he didn't want to break this fragile bond he could feel growing between them.

And he was very aware that he might be putting her in the awkward position of saying no to him while she was dependent on him. He would never hurt her and he hoped she understood that, but... no, now was not the right time. "Tell me about your family, your homeland."

"I grew up in a bayou—which is basically wetlands or swamp. My family is loud and large and while I love them... My sister and I never felt like we fit in."

"How so?"

"We just wanted different things, saw the world differently, I guess. My father was a drunk, my mom was always taking care of us. He could never hold a job which meant my mom had to hide what little money she made from him. Because if he found it, he'd take it and blow through it on cheap moonshine or whatever he could get his hands on." She shook her head, her tone almost dismissive, but he could feel the sadness rolling off her. The scent of it was sharp, potent.

"You don't have to talk about it."

"No, I kind of like opening up about this. It's been a long time. Unless this is too heavy to talk about?"

He shook his head, eager to learn everything about her, though he hated that her father hadn't been there to protect her the way a parent should.

"My dad died of liver failure when I was still in high school. Ah, I was a teenager. So I ended up picking up a lot of slack around the house, working two jobs to help my mom out. I always felt guilty when I'd buy art supplies for myself, but one of my aunts was a big support. When she realized how bad it was at our place, she engaged the whole family to help out. Because of that I was able to go to college and not feel guilty. Or as guilty," she added. "Eventually my sister moved out too and in with me in New Orleans. We sort of took care of each other after that, which was nice." She shrugged and he was under the impression she was done.

But then she surprised him by continuing. "Robin, my sister, she hated Charles. She didn't tell me at first because I was so smitten." Mia covered her face and groaned. "I know I shouldn't be embarrassed for making such a poor choice, but the way Charles was with me, was the way my dad had been with my mom to an extent. The love-bombing. The compliments and promises that turned out to be empty."

Sighing, she let her hand fall away. "Neptune never warmed up to him either, which should have been another sign." She paused, watching him curiously. "What about you? Any scary exes in your past?"

His mouth curved up as he shook his head. "No."

He wasn't going to tell her about his former lovers, few as they were. They were all warriors like him, had all been looking for quick comfort and pleasure, nothing more.

With Mia, he wanted so much more. He wanted forever, someone to share his life with, someone who cared about him as more than a warrior. Someone who loved... just him. He wanted to create something real with her.

"That's good," she murmured, and he could hear the exhaustion creeping into her voice.

"Come here," he growled, letting his protectiveness take over. "I can hear your teeth chattering. Just curl up against me until you get warm."

To his surprise, she didn't argue or push him away. Instead, she buried her face in his chest, and he was so glad he'd taken off his tunic.

He loved the feel of even her face touching his skin, though he wanted far more of her pressed against him, wrapped around him.

She slid her arm around him and sighed happily. "You're better than a fire." Her voice was fading now, and he knew it wouldn't be long until she finally dozed off.

He heard Ilmari nearby, making his way to the camp, likely glutted on too much meat and ready to pass out.

"Feel free to use me for my warmth." Or my cock, he silently added. Goddess, she could use him anytime, anywhere.

# CHAPTER 27

Mia was aware of a gentle hand on her shoulder, then a soft squeeze of pressure. "Mia, time to get up."

"I'm still asleep," she murmured without opening her eyes. Though she liked the sound of Tiber's deep voice, especially first thing in the morning.

Wait... she cracked open an eyelid, saw it was still dark out and pulled her blanket back over her head. "What time is it?"

A deep chuckle. "Early. Sun won't be up for an hour."

"If the sun isn't up then neither am I. Now shushy-shush. Sleepy time." She felt like she'd just fallen asleep and didn't want to get out of her warm cocoon.

Another chuckle. "I didn't realize you weren't a morning person."

"I'm a temperamental artist," she said semi-petulantly. "We don't concern ourselves with things like clocks and schedules. Let me sleep."

"We need to take to the skies before the storm rolls in. I'm worried Ilmari will struggle in rougher winds."

Well crap. Sighing, she shoved her blanket off her head and glared at him, but sat up, yawning. "I can't argue with that."

"I made you a mug of tea for travel. And a light breakfast."

"I guess I could eat." She was still a little whiny, but whatever, she wanted to sleep.

Ilmari was near the dwindling fire, sort of hopping back and forth excitedly, which made her smile. "You ready to fly?"

*Chirp, chirp!*

Okay then. Groaning at the world in general, she got up, headed off a ways for some privacy, took care of her morning business, then returned to find that Tiber had packed up everything of hers and was waiting with said tea in hand as well as a little cake.

A gorgeous man giving her food and tea? Yes, please.

"I'm sorry I had to wake you."

She eyed what turned out to be a small lemon cake that dragons seemed to love. "Since you're feeding me, I forgive you," she murmured, taking the cake with a yawn.

In that moment his gaze landed on her mouth, pure heat in his eyes for just a second. And she definitely hadn't imagined it.

But he turned away quickly, patting Ilmari on the back with a level of affection she wouldn't have expected from him months ago, then gave the little dragon a command in a language she didn't understand.

Ilmari certainly did because he flattened himself low to the ground so she could climb on easier with her food and drink.

"You're a perfect little baby," she whispered as she slid onto the seat/saddle contraption made for the little dragons.

She loved it because while she'd ridden Ilmari without the saddle, this felt more secure. Not that she was worried about Tiber letting anything happen to her, but it helped lower her anxiety as they flew.

"Here." Tiber approached again, his expression hard to read in the still dim light, but he held out a hooded cape and wrapped it around her, securing it at the front of her throat, his fingers skimming against her skin in the most delicious way. "You can cinch this if the wind gets to be too much and it will protect your face. But Ilmari knows where to fly to protect you from the wind."

Technically, Tiber's big dragon self was the one who protected her from the wind, but she knew what he meant.

She patted the thick hooded material with a smile. "Thank you. If it ends up raining and you want to push through, I'm okay with that."

"I'm not okay with that. But we'll see what happens."

She nodded, then averted her gaze as he stepped away and began stripping down to nothing. Every part of her wanted to watch his glorious body before he shifted to an even more stunning dragon, but it was way too early to get all hot and bothered. Especially after the way she'd slept curled up next to him all night. He'd been warm and wonderful... and she didn't have the right to watch him anyway. It would feel too intimate.

***

Mia squinted as the drops of icy rain started to splatter against her face and ducked down against Ilmari, who had already started to swoop lower.

Wind rushed over them as Ilmari made a sharp turn, heading down into what looked like a valley. She wasn't sure if they would have to worry about flooding or snow falls later.

But she could understand why Ilmari needed to land. She'd felt it the moment the air temperature had dropped and then the sudden splatters of rain that felt like little needles of ice striking her face.

Suddenly the rain slowed, then stopped and she realized that Tiber's beautiful amber-gold dragon was coasting above them, blocking them from the worst of it as Ilmari headed in for a landing.

When it didn't feel like he was landing fast enough, she ducked her head and closed her eyes, bracing for impact as they neared the flat-ish landing area Ilmari had chosen. She realized it wasn't a true valley, but an intermontane plateau between two mountains.

As soon as Ilmari came to a full stop, she realized how quiet it had gotten, the wind a dull howl instead of the raging from up above. It was still raining, but there was an overhang from the side of the mountain that would shelter them. It looked like there might be a cave too, but she couldn't tell with the shadows.

"Come on," she nudged her gray-scaled friend. "That way."

Ilmari hop-ran toward the covering, his running much bumpier than his flying. As they ducked under the dry cover, Tiber executed a perfect landing nearby.

He shifted so quickly from his giant beast, a burst of sparking magic exploding into the air before leaving the rough-hewn male crouched in the rain.

She stared, the sight of him in the pouring rain, completely naked, his body pure granite... that image was imprinted on her brain forever. Right then and there she decided that once she had access to supplies, she was going to paint him.

Even if she kept it for herself, he was too beautiful not to memorialize on canvas.

Somehow, she forced herself to unstrap and slide off Ilmari. Then she busied herself not looking at the very naked, gorgeous man she couldn't stop obsessing about.

Tiber was whisper quiet as he entered the overhang, carrying his own pack. She also realized he was now wearing pants (unfortunately). "We're not too far from the artist's sanctuary. If the storms don't let up, we'll have to go in the morning, but if this passes, we can head out before dark."

Mia walked to the edge of the overhang, standing back enough to be protected from the rain, but close enough that she could watch the harsh downfall. The sky was a mercurial gray, with streaks of lightning flashing every few seconds in the west.

But she realized they wouldn't have to worry about flooding as she watched a naturally carved canyon carry the heavy streams of water down over the side of the plateau.

"Stay here." Tiber's voice rolled over her as he stepped up next to her, so quietly she hadn't heard him. "I'm going to check out the interior of the cave."

She hadn't realized it was that deep but turned and watched as a swath of darkness swallowed him whole. Better him than her, because he was definitely the apex predator on this mountain.

Chilled, she wrapped her arms around herself even as Ilmari moved toward the edge of the overhang and shook his wings out, careful not to hit her.

Then he chirped animatedly at her as he hopped around the edge of the cave, sniffing at the walls curiously.

She briefly wondered what he was smelling, but then got to work unrolling both Tiber's and her bedrolls near a long cold firepit. He'd taken care of her last night, and she wanted to get things ready this time.

By the time he walked out of the darkness, she had already set up their bedding, started a small fire and had a pot of tea going.

"You didn't have to do all this," he murmured, frowning at her.

She shrugged, wondering if anyone had ever taken care of him at all. Then she silenced her curiosity because she didn't want to imagine some gorgeous dragon female with him. "I'm making the tea a little sweeter." Just the way he liked it. She'd noticed he added sugar to his, so she was brewing this pot differently to make it sweeter to begin with.

"Thank you. The cave is empty, just a few old packs and blankets in the back from fellow travelers."

She'd already draped her hooded wrap on a rock to dry and sat cross-legged by the fire, sighing in enjoyment at the warmth. "I'm really glad it's you escorting me and not a stranger," she said as she looked at the crackling fire. "This trip is a lot different than I imagined."

"There's a way to go on foot, but it would take you almost a month."

"I prefer this... even if it's a little terrifying. And exhilarating," she added. "I never imagined any of this in my entire life."

"Dragons?"

"Dragons, different realms, all of it. I think I told you that I already knew about some supernaturals before The Fall, but this is next level. Traveling with a dragon—two dragons," she added when Ilmari chirped indignantly from where he continued to sniff along the wall's edge.

Tiber watched her across the fire, shadows playing over his face and making it hard to read his expression. He looked as if he was about to say something, but a harsh cry filled the air, making her wince.

Before she could think about moving, he was at the cave's entrance, his expression hard in profile. "I'm going to go check that out. Stay put."

"You don't have to tell me twice," she murmured as another cry, this one more of a screech, filled the air. Cool fingers skated over her spine as he headed out into the icy wetness.

She knew that he was more than capable of taking care of himself and probably a whole squadron of dragons, but she still worried as he took to the skies and disappeared into falling sheets of rain.

Shivering, she stepped back into the safety of the cave and started rummaging around for a way to make the cave more inviting when he returned.

But when Ilmari started chirping wildly and raced out into the rain, she ran after him—and came face to face with a terrifying creature out of her nightmares.

# CHAPTER 28

At the sound of Mia screaming, Tiber abruptly turned, shooting through the air faster than he'd ever flown. He used the flow of wind to his advantage as he soared up over the plateau only to see an altomayudo carrying Mia up the side of the mountain.

Rage and fear punched through him in a way he'd never experienced.

Ilmari chirped pitifully from the ground, his wing clearly injured.

Tiber would take care of him later, all his focus on Mia as he arrowed straight for the beast.

With a humanoid body, feathery wings, and a face with six bulging black eyes, the flying beast was known for its viciousness.

When it spotted Tiber flying straight for it, it released Mia from its talons with a savage screech and flew straight up in the air, knowing it would lose in a battle against Tiber.

He dove straight toward Mia as she plummeted toward the earth. She wasn't even screaming, but as he arrowed straight for her, he could see the fear etched into her face as she watched him flying at her.

Keeping pace, he swooped in underneath her, felt the moment when she landed on his back with a yelp. He slowed immediately as he flew downward, spreading his wings to slow their descent. Though it only took minutes, time seemed to stretch for an eternity until he landed next to Ilmari.

Before he'd even tucked his wings in, she was scrambling off him and racing for the dragonling. And by the time he'd shifted, she was already crouched down next to the chirping little beast.

Tears tracked down her face as she murmured soothing words to him. "You're going to be okay, you have to be."

"He's going to be fine," Tiber murmured, scooping his arms under Ilmari. The hold was awkward, but he could easily transport him back to the cave. "His wing is sprained, but he should be able to fly tomorrow. If not, I'll carry you both."

"I can't believe you're carrying him now." Her teeth were chattering, her face pale as she hurried alongside him.

And goddess, he wanted to comfort her, but they needed to get Ilmari out of the open and settled so he could rest and heal.

Once he got Ilmari next to the fire, he worked quickly to stretch the little one's wing to the right angle. "The ointment in the green bottle," he said as Mia opened his small kit.

They worked together to rub the healing salve where he could see Ilmari had been injured the worst. Likely tossed against the side of the mountain given the scratches.

"I know I shouldn't have left the cave, but that... thing, attacked Ilmari. He was just trying to protect me and it shook him like a ragdoll, then threw him down. You were so brave though," she whispered to Ilmari, who was making sad little chirping sounds. "The bravest dragon that ever lived."

Ilmari sniffed slightly, then nudged his head up against her hand for comfort as Tiber continued to set the wing. Dragons and dragonlings healed quickly, but... "You'll have to remain still tonight, Ilmari. No hopping around. If you do that, you'll be fine in the morning."

Ilmari chirped, then nudged Tiber's hand as if to say thank you.

"What was that thing?" Mia asked, her voice shaking, traces of fear lingering in her words as she got some of the dried snacks out for Ilmari.

"Altomayudo. They're not normally in this territory, so either something is hunting it, or it got separated from its flock. Maybe both."

She shuddered. "It was creepy looking. All those eyes."

Creepy was one word for it. Dead was another, because Tiber was going to find it and kill it later. But he kept that thought to himself as he scanned Mia's face.

Goddess, she looked terrified. "Come here," he ordered, belatedly realizing he still didn't have any clothes on.

But she didn't seem to notice or care as she basically threw herself in his arms. That's when he knew how afraid she was. He was kneeling as she buried her face against his neck. He held her close, inwardly cursing the animal that had almost taken her from him.

"You're okay." He kept his voice low, soothing, as he gently rubbed a hand up and down her spine.

Her fingers dug into his back as she held him tight, her breathing evening out until he finally stood, but kept his hold on her.

As she looked up at him now, without thinking, he cupped her cheeks and began to wipe away her tears—but stilled when she sucked in a sharp breath.

It took him a moment to recognize the scent rolling off her as she stared up at him, her green eyes wide, searching as she watched him. No longer was the acrid scent of fear filling the cave, but something sweeter, deeper.

Lust.

"Mia." Her name tore from his throat as he cupped her jaw, leaned down slowly, closing the distance between them.

He didn't want to stop, but he wouldn't take advantage of her. Never. But definitely not now when she had to be feeling vulnerable.

To his surprise, she grabbed onto his shoulders and leaned up on her toes, closing the distance between them.

That was all he needed to take over, to crush his mouth to hers in a raw claiming.

Goddess, she tasted sweet and perfect, and instead of being timid, she kissed him hard and with abandon, pressing her body up against his as they learned each other.

When she playfully nipped his bottom lip, he groaned against her mouth, then lifted her up so she could wrap her legs around him.

He'd never been this hard in his entire life, his cock steel between his legs, but when Ilmari suddenly chirped wildly, they broke apart.

Mia was breathless, her eyes slightly unfocused as she blinked and looked over at the dragonling.

Who was looking at them in what Tiber could only describe as pure disgust.

Mia snickered, then buried her face against Tiber's chest. "Pretty sure he's grossed out by us. I can't even look at him."

Ilmari chirped in the affirmative.

Goddess, Tiber wanted to tell Ilmari to just shut his eyes if he didn't like it, then drag Mia deeper into the cave and taste the sweetness between her legs until she was crying out his name.

Then he wanted to do it again until all she knew was pleasure, until his name was the only one she ever thought of. It took a long moment for him to settle, to get himself under control as he continued to hold her close.

"This was probably a mistake anyway," she said, pulling away from him on a sigh.

Mistake? Oh no. His instinct was to yank her back to him, but he didn't give into his more primal urge. Mia was human, physically weaker than him. And right now, it was just the three of them on this mountain, with potential threats out there.

He clearly scented her desire, but he never wanted her to feel pressure when it came to him. Still, kissing her could never be a mistake. It was just the beginning.

"This was not a mistake," he growled, before stalking out of the cave into the cold rain.

# CHAPTER 29

*Dear Robin,*

*I think I've officially lost it because I'm falling for Tiber. He's nothing like I originally assumed and now that we've kissed, I can't get his taste out of my mind. Or the feel of him against me. And yes, I know that's TMI, but I don't even know if I'll send this letter. I just know that I have to get this out! (Oh yeah, we kissed, another news flash!)*

*He's acting as my guide as we leave the territory until Charles has gone, though he made it clear that he wants to "take care of Charles." Is it terrible that I don't want to question what he means too closely?*

*You'll know this long before you get this letter, but he's also sent people to watch out for you in New Orleans in case Charles decides to hurt me through the one I love the most.*

*Tomorrow morning, we head out for the artist's retreat, and I must admit I'm excited to finally make it, especially after the adventure from today. A giant beast scooped me up and flew away with me and likely would have killed me or eaten me but Tiber swooped in and saved me. Oh, I probably should have led with that in my letter. But the kiss stands out more than the wildest scare of my life.*

*I hope you're doing well and hope to send this once I return. All my love.*

*Xo,*
*Mia*

# CHAPTER 30

Mia looked up from the fire as Tiber finally stalked back into the cave. He'd been in and out for the last hour trying to decide if they should head out before sunset or not.

And also, she was pretty sure he was grumpy because Ilmari had insisted they stop making out. Which, fair. She was a little annoyed too—but also maybe grateful. She didn't think kissing him was a mistake, but she could have easily gotten carried away.

She hadn't realized that Ilmari had that much awareness. She'd assumed that he was more like Neptune, but now she knew. There was so much about this realm, and supernaturals and their customs she was learning on a daily basis.

"So what's the verdict?" she asked.

"It'll be dark soon enough and the sky still looks too temperamental. I say we hunker down and leave in the morning."

"I'm fine with that." There was no sense in pushing themselves, especially when Tiber would have to carry both of them at this point.

Ilmari, who had scooted up next to her and stretched his set wing out around her in a protective embrace chirped a little haughtily at Tiber.

Mia wasn't sure how to translate it, but Tiber simply grunted at the dragonling. He'd assured her that Ilmari would be fine by morning, that he healed faster than what she was used to, and she was glad for it.

Suddenly Tiber straightened, then held his finger up to his mouth as he looked at the two of them, before disappearing into the growing twilight beyond the mouth of the cave.

Minutes later she heard a whooshing sound, then male laughter.

She straightened slightly but knew Tiber would protect them from anything. Though she was surprised when moments later he strode into the cave with two large males who were likely dragons. Or bears. But given the territory, her money was on them being dragons.

They both stopped and stared at her in surprise, then more surprise when they saw Ilmari, who was growling low in his throat. Definitely not his normal purring.

Oh. She blinked at Ilmari, wondering if she should be wary too.

"They're okay, Ilmari." Tiber's voice was soothing. "These are not enemies."

Ilmari immediately stilled, but scooted closer to Mia.

And her heart melted a little bit more. This sweet baby dragon was so protective it was hard not to want to cuddle him close and give him all the treats he wanted.

"Mia, this is Kirkurte. He trained under me long ago before moving on to bigger things." The male had dark hair pulled back in small braids against his skull with little beads at the ends of them.

On second glance she realized that they weren't beads but looked more like bone fragments. Oh my. Despite the cold weather, he wore loose pants, no shirt, and carried a small pack with him. His skin was a beautiful bronze that seemed to glow even in the dimness of the cave.

She nodded politely at him even as Tiber introduced the other male.

"And this is Cordro." He didn't say how he knew the other male with pale blond hair that looked almost silver. He was dressed similarly to Kirkurte, but had a plethora of tattoos covering his olive-hued skin.

"Pleasure to meet you both."

"The pleasure is all ours," Kirkurte said, stepping further into the cave. "I've never met a human before."

Mia wasn't sure how to respond as she looked between the two men who were just as large as Tiber. He seemed at ease with them, and he'd told Ilmari they weren't enemies, so that was something.

But a part of her she wanted to ignore was annoyed by their presence, that they'd interrupted them. Because she'd been enjoying this time with Tiber in a way she'd never expected. Still, she smiled at Kirkurte politely. "So what brings you here? Do you live near these mountains?"

"No, indeed. We're just traveling and got caught up in some lightning." Kirkurte shrugged dismissively and set his pack down next to the fire, then sat. "Figured it was better to wait out the storm instead of trying to fly through it."

Tiber sat on her other side so that he and Ilmari bracketed her in. She wanted to lean into him, to take advantage of his warmth, but wasn't sure he would welcome it, especially in front of the newcomers.

That little insecurity she'd been trying to bury bubbled up again. It was one thing to kiss her in private but that meant nothing at all. She was a human in a cave with powerful dragons. Perhaps Tiber wouldn't want the others to even guess that they'd been intimate.

Cordro nodded along with his friend and as he sat, dug into his own bag. Then he pulled out a smaller one filled with dried meats and fruits. "Here, we just picked these up this morning if you are hungry, human." He leaned around the fire to hand her what looked like dried apples or something similar. "They're quite sweet and don't suit us. But I've heard humans like this kind of thing."

Surprising her, Tiber snatched the bag away from his friend and tucked it next to him. "You don't give her food."

Kirkurte's mouth fell open for a moment while Cordro blinked rapidly.

"Is it poison?" she blurted before she could censor herself.

"Oh sweet goddess," Kirkurte murmured, a grin on his face. "Not poison, sweetheart."

The sweetheart got a growl from Tiber.

And then Ilmari chirped indignantly at Tiber, chittering away so quickly that Mia could only stare.

Tiber looked at the others after listening to the dragonling, his expression dry. "But Ilmari will accept your offering of sweets," he said before he opened the bag and set the dried fruit in front of Ilmari.

Mia would have loved the dried fruit but kept the thought to herself as she glanced sideways at Tiber. He'd said these males weren't enemies, but all his muscles were pulled taut, and he looked ready to attack at a moment's notice.

"So tell us why you're out here in this vast land with two wild dragons," Kirkurte said, grinning at Mia.

"Oh, I'm on a journey to an artist's retreat for inspiration and hope to get some work in. Tiber graciously offered to be my guide."

Kirkurte looked between the two of them. "Guide, huh?"

"He's an excellent guide," Cordro added, nodding solemnly. But he looked as if he might be fighting a smile.

She frowned at the two of them. Were they messing with Tiber? "Yes, he is. And he saved my life. I'm very grateful to have him with me." She sniffed slightly at the two of them, not sure about their tones.

"Wait, are you the Mia who Princess Stella sponsored?" Cordro asked suddenly. When she nodded, he continued. "Goddess, I've heard nothing but wonderful things about your work..."

As she fell into a conversation with him, both Tiber and Kirkurte disappeared outside the cave, talking in hushed tones.

She missed his presence immediately, but found that this Cordro had an artistic bent and was a pleasure to talk to. As they talked, she wondered where Tiber had gotten off to, but felt too awkward to ask if the other man knew.

Because it was clear that he and Kirkurte had left the area. When she yawned for the tenth time, Cordo smiled gently.

"Don't let me keep you up. They shouldn't be gone much longer. Please feel free to bed down. I'll wait outside for them to give you privacy."

"I am really tired," she admitted.

Ilmari had dozed not too long ago, snoring softly next to her.

Cordro stood and nodded. "I'll be out there if you need me."

She was a little surprised by how polite he was, but grateful he was giving her privacy. She might find his conversation enjoyable but didn't want to fall asleep next to a stranger.

She wasn't even sure she would fall asleep at all, but sometime later, she was aware of Tiber slipping into the bedroll next to her.

The firelight was dim, but he was pure heat as he wrapped his arm around her and pulled her back to his chest.

"Where'd you go?" she murmured, setting her hand over his. Maybe later she'd think about how easy it was to cuddle up with him, or how sensual this position could be under different circumstances, but for now she was simply grateful he was back.

"Taking care of something."

"What?" she asked, her voice fading again as the lure of sleep pulled her under. She was safe in Tiber's arms, knew that he would protect both her and Ilmari.

Instead of responding, she felt him kiss the back of her head and murmur something in a language she'd never heard. Even the translating spell she'd undergone before entering the territory did nothing to make sense of it.

But she leaned back into him and savored his tight hold and dark, delicious scent that wrapped around her.

# CHAPTER 31

"Never thought I'd see the great Tiber fall for a wisp of a woman." Kirkurte was grinning as he and Cordro readied to leave outside the cave.

Mia was still sleeping inside with Ilmari, and Tiber wanted to let her sleep as long as possible before waking her.

Cordro snickered slightly as he pulled out another bag of dried fruit. "I'm officially giving this to you so if you give it to her, it's a gift from you, not another male." His tone was amused.

Though Tiber wanted to ignore it, he'd seen the way Mia had glanced at the bag, interest in her green eyes. "Thank you for the gift," he ground out.

Which made the two of them laugh in unison.

But then Kirkurte straightened slightly. "Is it... difficult with a human? With her being so different physically?"

Protectiveness swelled inside him even though the other man hadn't insulted her. "She's one of the most talented and kind people I know. The realm is lucky to have her presence." Him more than anyone, even if he hadn't claimed her yet. But after yesterday, he couldn't deny it any longer.

She was his.

"I wasn't insulting her." Kirkurte raised his palms slightly, a grin playing at his mouth. "I was just curious. She is quite attractive. I only wondered if perhaps she had human friends or a sister and—"

"Sweet Goddess," Cordro muttered. "He's going to take off your head. And you'll deserve it."

"She does have a sister," Tiber said. "And I'll make sure to warn her against you. Where are you two headed anyway?" Dawn had just broken and there weren't any storm clouds in sight.

But around here, he knew that could change in an instant.

"To the castle. Starlena recalled us for a while." Cordro shrugged. "Said she might have use of us."

That was news to him, but not a surprise.

"Good. While you're there, perhaps you can do me a favor."

"Anything," Kirkurte murmured practically in unison with Cordro.

He laid out why they'd left and as many details as he thought were pertinent about Charles and his coven. When he was done, they both nodded, their expressions dark.

"We'll keep our ear to the ground," Cordro said.

"Indeed. Now unless you want to see my glorious cock and weep for how lacking you are, I'm going to strip and shift now," Kirkurte said.

Tiber rolled his eyes as he said, "Safe travels," but didn't smother his laugh as he headed back inside. It had been an age since he'd seen the two of them and he hoped they'd still be at the castle when he returned.

More than that, he hoped Charles was gone so he could get about the business of hunting him down in New Orleans and taking care of him for good.

# CHAPTER 32

Octavia soared high in the air above one of Nova's portals, watching while camouflaged as the vampire coven spoke with the two dragons who guarded the portal.

She'd promised Tiber she would watch the asshole Charles leave with her own eyes and she wouldn't let him down. She'd have done this anyway for Mia. The human was kind in a way she hadn't expected.

That was mostly based on her own biases, but some truth from what she'd heard of humans from reputable sources. She should have known better, however, considering one of their own princesses now lived in the human realm and was thriving there.

In a place called New Orleans she hoped to visit one day. Perhaps Mia would give her some tips on things to do while there. She watched as the vampires finally crossed the portal. The flash of light indicating their exit, the last thing she needed to see.

She turned away, heading toward the stronghold where she needed to meet with Cyprus and unfortunately, Nolan.

He'd been a beast to deal with ever since the party and had kept asking about Asa, clearly jealous of him. Yet Nolan hadn't made a move on her.

And while she had no problem making a move when it came to sex, she wouldn't when it came to her future mate.

They were dragons, he had to chase her, and it was clear that he wasn't going to. So she was doing what she always did, compartmentalizing her feelings.

Hell, she'd been doing it since she was a dragonling found abandoned on a floating block of ice in the middle of a dead realm.

She had no idea who her family was or where she came from.

And it didn't bother her anymore. She had her family.

She'd just thought maybe... she might get more. But it seemed as if that kind of life wasn't for her. She wasn't going to get to build a future with someone or have dragonlings of her own. And she would eventually be okay with that.

Thanks to a strong tailwind, it didn't take long to reach the stronghold.

Cyprus, Angel, Nolan and Juno were all waiting in the meeting room for her.

"Vampires are gone," she said as she strode in, not making eye contact with Nolan because it hurt too much. "What do I need to know?" She kept her focus on Cyprus.

"Starlena made contact. We might have a problem in the north."

# CHAPTER 33

*Three days later*

Was it possible to crawl out of your skin from sexual frustration? Mia was almost certain it was. She'd been at the most beautiful, secluded artist's retreat for three days and Tiber hadn't kissed her once.

Had barely touched her at all. It was almost as if he was ignoring her.

And maybe that made her a contrarian but she only wanted him more.

"Whatever you're sketching, I love the ragey vibe," Aki said as she approached Mia.

She'd set up in the large studio the painters of the group tended to use. There was also a studio for sculptors and then a much larger one for what she would have called mixed media back home.

The artist's retreat was like nothing she'd ever been to before. On the top of a small mountain (small being relative, but compared to the beasts surrounding it, it was), an enclave of stone and wood homes in random shapes created a makeshift circle, with the various studios in the middle of everything. And all the little homes had tons of glass for natural light and inviting porches encouraging the artists to interact with each other. They also had indoor plumbing, something she was grateful for. She'd been on retreats before in mountainous or desert areas and they'd all stayed in tents and basically roughed it.

Mia could admit that she liked her creature comforts and modern conveniences.

She looked up from her canvas, where she'd started sketching the scary beast from days ago and gave Aki a wry smile. "I'm not sure what I want to work on and I think it's making me a little manic."

"Go relax then. Or hike, or check out the springs or... anything. You're here to reconnect with nature. You don't have to work if you don't want."

"I feel like I should say something cheesy like painting isn't work." It was, technically. Because her paintings took time and effort, but they also fed her soul.

"It's work that fills us up," she said, mirroring Mia's own thoughts.

Aki, an avian shifter of some kind, grinned. Her midnight dark hair was pulled up into a long braid and she wore a cream-colored sweater with loose wool pants. Her feet were bundled into thick boots, and her scarf was wrapped around her neck three times, telling Mia that she wasn't as warm-blooded as dragon shifters at all.

They'd met months ago at Xenia's gallery right as Aki was about to leave on her journey here, and she simply adored the other woman.

"I saw that big dragon of yours heading for the springs. Maybe you can catch him."

She didn't correct Aki to tell her that Tiber wasn't hers. Because she didn't want anyone else coming on to him while they were here. "The springs, really?"

Tiber had been working nonstop since they'd arrived; fixing one of the kilns, then securing two of the homes built off the side of the mountain to make sure they would remain secure, and about fifty other small jobs that had piled up. He'd been working from before she woke up, until after sunset. He'd joined her and the others for tea and breakfast this morning, but then he'd disappeared when she hadn't been looking. He'd barely said a word to anyone except to ask for what needed fixing.

"I'm just as surprised as you that he took a break," Aki said with a laugh. She glanced around, then lowered her voice to a whisper. "No one else will be there if you two want some alone time."

Only one way to find out if he actually wanted alone time with her. She couldn't ask for a better opportunity. "Maybe I will join him."

She set her pencil down on the ledge of her easel and pushed back in her seat. She'd been mindlessly drawing anyway, just trying to get inspired for her next work, when she wanted nothing more than to get naked with Tiber.

If he regretted their kiss, then fine, he could at least tell her, not ignore her. As she made her way to her cabin, she waved at Ilmari who was posing for one of the other artists, one wing up in a silly pose. He gave her a little wave and chirped happily before going back to his "serious face."

At least one of them was having a good time here.

In her cabin she stripped off her clothes, then slipped on her thick robe and slippers, twisted her hair up into a bun and headed out. It was cold up here, but not icily so. The way this place had been carved out somehow avoided whipping winds. Not to mention the hot springs added to the luxury of it. There was one hot round-ish spring half the size of an Olympic pool, then fifteen more below it that were basically stacked on top of each other along one of the mountainsides. Each small pool was cerulean blue with white puffs of steam rolling off them. Someone had built a railing at the very bottom of the final three pools, likely for any non-shifters and she was grateful for the extra security.

She followed the magically lit stone steps past the last house, anticipation building in her as she made her way to the springs and hopefully Tiber.

But disappointment punched into her when she reached the big pool and didn't see him anywhere. As she set her towel down, however, she heard the faintest rustle and out of the corner of her eye saw him shimmying down from one of the higher rock faces. He was in human form but she had no idea what he might be doing. Even so, she decided to take the opportunity to lure him into one of the pools.

Or that was the plan.

She'd never been a seductress, but she was tired of whatever was going on between them. If he made a move now, she'd know. And if not, then she'd also know—and drown herself in sweet treats later.

Feeling bolder than she ever had, she dropped her robe onto one of the lounge chairs and strode naked to the big pool. Her nipples tightened under the cooler air, but more than that, she could feel Tiber's hot stare on her.

Maybe it was wishful thinking, but she swore he tracked her every step as she approached the bigger pool, slipped off her sandals and then slid into blessed heat.

She sighed as the warmth enveloped her even as she hoped he would follow her. She swam to the far edge and looked below at the rest of the pools, all stacked on top of each other in a little waterfall of color. Whoever had designed the pools was brilliant.

"Mia." The deep timbre of Tiber's voice made her turn and she realized he was only a few feet away from her.

"Finally taking a break?" Her words came out far more tartly than she'd intended, but come on, she'd been aching for him ever since that kiss.

He blinked in clear surprise, then his amber-gold eyes narrowed ever so slightly. "Are you upset with me?"

"Just wondering why you've been ignoring me for three days."

He blinked again, somehow still surprised. Seriously, how was this a surprise to him?

"Look, I get it if you regret our kiss, but—"

He moved faster than she could track, pinning her up against the edge of the pool and oh... oooh, he was rock hard, his erection insistently pressing against her abdomen.

She sucked in a breath at the feel of his reaction, glad she wasn't the only one feeling this chemistry, this connection.

"I could never regret kissing you." His voice was a deep rumble as he leaned down, buried his face in her neck and inhaled.

Warmth flooded between her legs at the way he was breathing her in while barely touching her—his erection notwithstanding because sweet honeysuckle, he was thick. But everything about this was intimate and real.

Feeling out of her depth, she slid her fingers up over his chest and savored the way he shuddered under her touch. "Why have you been ignoring me?" she whispered.

Raising his head, he looked down at her, all heat and hunger. "I've been trying to give you space," he practically gritted out.

"Space?" When had she asked for that?

"I didn't want you to feel crowded or pressured." Again, he seemed to be trying to force the words out, as if he was holding onto his control.

"I didn't ask for space." And please, he could crowd up against her anytime he wanted. Her nipples beaded even tighter at the feel of all this skin to skin, at the way he was pinning her in place as if he was afraid she'd bolt.

"I... am aware of the physical differences between us. I'm trying to..."

She wasn't sure what he wanted to say but could guess. "You're worried that I'll freak out if we have sex and then expect more?" she murmured, sliding her hand down lower, lower, until she skated her fingers over the head of his thick length. They could enjoy each other without getting hung up on the future or commitment. Maybe he was worried she'd be all clingy?

He shuddered, his amber-gold eyes starting to glow.

"I promise I'm okay with just having fun with you. No promises or expectations. Just fun." Okay, she was lying a little because she wanted more than that, but it was clear that he was worried about her. Probably because she was human. But she wanted him and it was clear that he wanted her. There was no reason they couldn't enjoy some pleasure for a while.

He growled low in his throat as he crushed his mouth to hers. But instead of pinning her against the hard wall, he wrapped his arm around her to block her back from scraping against the stone.

She didn't even have to think about it, she wanted to touch him everywhere. Instead of just teasing him, she wrapped her fingers around his thick length and started to stroke, but he pulled back, breathing hard before she could get into it.

"Not yet." Another growl, this one more pained as he took her hand, and slid it up to his shoulder. "No touching... yet." His eyes were still glowing and she wanted to ask him about it.

But she was way more interested in the way his other hand was dipping between her legs, exploring, and teasing and ooooh—she clutched onto his shoulders hard as he dipped a finger inside her. Slowly, teasingly, tentatively at first.

"You're so wet already." His lips were a soft caress against hers.

She couldn't respond, simply tightened around him on a moan.

"Fuck, you're gorgeous. Later, you'll come against my face."

Her inner walls clenched again, and he smiled.

"You like the thought of that." A soft, raspy whisper.

All she could do was nod and arch her breasts against his chest, because yes, she wanted to come against his face. And his cock, and his fingers. And anywhere else he wanted.

Smiling darkly, he captured her mouth again as he added another thick digit inside her.

She moaned into his mouth, her entire body one raw nerve as he slowly began sliding his fingers inside her, teasing, stretching, oh yes please, he started rubbing her clit with his thumb. It didn't matter that it was too soon.

Way too soon. Normally it took so much longer for her to be able to come. She needed lots of foreplay and patience.

But the way he was kissing her and teasing her—and the fact that it was Tiber—she knew it wouldn't be long. She rolled her hips against the movement of his fingers, nipping at his bottom lip as he continued pleasuring her.

She was vaguely aware of him pulling her away from the wall and realized why when he used his other hand to cup her breast, gently rolling her hard nipple between his thumb and forefinger.

But he followed it up with a pinch that had her tightening around him even harder.

"Come for me now, just a little pleasure before the main course," he whispered against her mouth, basically ordering her to come. "Then I'm going to bend you over and take you from behind."

She jolted at his words, the image of him taking her like that sending her into orgasm. She hadn't even realized she'd been ready, but his words sent a ribbon of pleasure punching through her. Combined with his wicked, talented fingers and the way he was teasing her breasts, she couldn't hold back as the climax surged through her. Her clit was swollen as she came and came and—he pulled out his fingers and she cried out at the loss. No, she was still coming.

But he moved fast, turning her around while still holding her close. "I'll try to be gentle."

Using his arm to balance in front of her and protect her from the stone, he slid his finger inside her again as he bent her over the pool's edge.

Still ultra-sensitive, her inner walls fluttered around him.

Leaning down, he nipped her earlobe. "You want this?"

"Yes, yes." Did she sound like she was begging? Who cared, she wanted him more than she'd ever wanted anyone. She was still shaking from his fingers alone, her inner walls feeling empty now, needing more. Needing the full length of him pushing inside her.

"Say you want my cock." He stroked his hard length over her back, then down between her thighs, making her moan again.

"Yes, I want you inside me. Stop teasing me," she rasped out, her words unsteady.

He spread her legs even farther apart, and eased his thick length into her. Below her the other springs rippled from the waterfall above, but oh god, all she could focus on was the way he was stretching her.

Filling her completely. "Oh god."

"*Tiber.*" He bent over her, nipping at her earlobe as he filled her to the hilt. "I want to hear *my* name on your lips. Say you'll never let anyone else touch you."

His dark, possessive words sent a thrill down her spine. "*Tiber.* No one else will touch me... Oh go—Tiber." She wasn't sure what she said after that, once he started thrusting into her from behind in long, hard strokes.

He gripped one of her hips hard, pinning her in place as he teased one of her nipples into a little pleasure point that bordered on painful.

All the while he thrust into her over and over until she found herself coming again, this time much harder than before. He'd been right, the one before had been a little appetizer.

This... pleasure punched out to all her nerve endings in a tidal wave, nearly sucking her under until stars seemed to spark in front of her as she came down from her high.

And then he was coming inside her, his strokes wild and unsteady as he found his own release. He murmured things in a language she couldn't understand, burying his face against her neck and scraping his teeth over a sensitive spot that had her tightening even more around him.

She wasn't sure how long he remained holding her after he came, but eventually he turned her around to face him and pulled her tight to his chest as he nuzzled her neck. "Goddess, you're perfect."

Feeling weak, but beyond sated, she stroked her fingers through his hair as he continued to pepper kisses along her jaw. "That was amazing," she whispered.

He nipped her in response and she swore she felt his cock getting thick again against her abdomen.

"Your eyes were glowing," she continued.

He went still for a moment before his fingers flexed on her hip, his hold oh so possessive. "It's a dragon thing," he murmured, before he took her mouth again.

She swore he was holding something back but couldn't imagine what it was. And as they kissed, she didn't much care.

# CHAPTER 34

Tiber pulled Mia's back close to his chest as he felt her starting to wake up. After taking her yesterday in the springs, then again in her cabin multiple times, she'd passed out some time last evening—after he'd insisted she eat.

Because his female needed her strength.

Before yesterday he hadn't understood what the mating instinct did to a dragon. He *thought* he'd understood, but after tasting her, feeling her come around his cock, hearing the moans of pleasure she made and his name on her lips as she reached the heights of pleasure, he knew he would never let her go.

A compulsion like he'd never imagined demanded that he claim her, mark her, bite her. But he knew it was too soon.

*Not too soon.*

He ignored his inner beast, found himself smiling as Mia pushed her ass back against him with intent.

"Someone's happy to see me this morning," she murmured, still in that peaceful, not-quite-awake phase.

He nipped her shoulder as he slid his palm down her stomach before cupping her mound, began teasing the hidden little bundle of nerves.

She jerked back against him with a gasp. "I can't believe you're ready to go again."

"With you, always." He bit down again, careful not to break her skin as he continued stroking her. "Are you ready?" he murmured even as he nudged her thighs up from behind with his own.

Then he slid his hard length between her thighs, rubbing along her folds and over her clit.

She sucked in a breath as the head of his cock slid over her nerves, so he did it again and again until she was breathing hard and reaching back to clutch his hip.

"I'm ready," she rasped out, her fingers digging into him.

"Maybe I'm not." He nipped her again. "Maybe I like teasing you."

Her breathing was unsteady as she reached between her legs and teased her own clit. "Maybe I'll get myself off."

Loving the challenging note in her voice, he grasped her wrist and pulled her hand away even as he slid into her from behind.

He growled against her neck as he filled her, thrusting slowly at first, enjoying each little gasp and moan she made. And he was fairly certain she loved the way he was restraining her wrist, wondered if she would enjoy more restraints later.

At that thought, he nipped her earlobe, wishing he could officially bite and claim her so that everyone would know she was taken. So they would be linked forever.

But that was something he could never take. *Would* never take. She was giving him her trust by being so vulnerable with him and it was something he would never betray.

When she'd mentioned his glowing eyes, he'd known without a doubt that she was his. Mating manifestations showed themselves in different ways for different dragons and his clan only ever showed their manifestation in a single way. Through their eyes.

"Tiber." There was a needy thread in her voice, so he released her wrist and began massaging her clit as he continued thrusting inside her.

And that was all it took for his Mia to lose control.

She shoved back against him with abandon as he lost himself inside her, her orgasm sharp and fast—allowing him to let go of his own control.

Control that had once been legendary at least in battle. But with her, it might as well not exist. There was nothing he wouldn't give her or do for her. "Mia." Her name was a prayer on his lips as they both came down from the bliss of climax.

When he rolled her onto her back and went to kiss her, she covered her mouth with an adorable little squeak.

"What are you doing?"

"I need to brush my teeth." Her words were garbled under her palm.

"I don't care about that."

"But I do."

"Can I kiss your breasts then?" he asked even as he slid down to her chest and began worshipping her.

In response, she laughed, which turned into a moan until they were both sated once again.

As they laid there in the dim morning light breaking through the drapes, he held her against his chest, memorizing this moment. Wanting to remember all of it.

He'd never felt so at peace as when he was with her. Not in a thousand years had he ever felt like this, and he wasn't certain he could put it into words, but she filled a place inside him he hadn't realized was missing.

"You better watch out or I won't let you go," she murmured against his chest, her words a little drowsy and he had a feeling she would doze before they headed to breakfast.

He snorted softly. Let him go? Perhaps she didn't understand, it was he who was never letting her go. But before he could respond, there was a rough banging on her cabin door.

He jolted up before Mia had even moved, hurrying to the front door and wrenching it open.

Her friend Aki stood on the other side, her eyes widening when she saw him standing there naked. Looking away quickly, she said, "I'm so sorry to interrupt you, but a friend of yours is here to see you, said it's important."

"They better be dying," he growled before he slammed the door on her.

# CHAPTER 35

"Octavia, what a nice surprise," Mia said as she hugged her.

Tiber simply wanted to knock his friend's head off. "Yes, what a lovely surprise."

Mia glanced at him in surprise, likely at his biting tone.

But he couldn't even hide his annoyance, not when his future mate had been naked in his arms mere minutes ago.

Octavia, who could definitely scent the sex and mating on them, held up her palms. "I sincerely apologize. I didn't mean for Aki to interrupt... you two. But congratulations," she said, looking between the two of them with a genuine smile.

"Ah..." Mia laughed awkwardly and glanced at Tiber, but he didn't respond to Octavia's words.

He certainly wasn't going to tell Mia they were in the midst of mating. Oh no. She would figure it out after she was so addicted to him, she wouldn't want to walk away. He was a sneaky dragon, after all.

"What do you want?" he demanded of his friend instead.

"Two things. The vampire and his coven are gone," she said, looking between the two of them. "I watched them leave the realm."

Mia's sigh of relief was audible and he pulled her close, wanting to anchor her.

"That did not require your flight here."

"No." Octavia's expression turned grim. "Starlena sent a message to the guard. There's trouble brewing in the north. We don't know the extent, but the realm has been breached by a small band of raiders. Right now, they're simply camped out near one of our strongholds. Cyprus and I have already sent out sentries to spy and assess the situation as Starlena requested, but I wanted to tell you in person."

Tiber nodded in agreement, annoyance gone. She'd been right to come. She could have sent a message through a spell. Unlike humans and their phones, this realm could send messages via magic, but often there was a cost, and they didn't always translate properly. And the flight wouldn't have been long for Octavia—it had only been extended for him because he'd paced himself with Mia and Ilmari. "Thank you. Let me discuss things with Mia and I'll let you know what the plan is. But grab breakfast and prepare Ilmari if he wants to leave with us. If he does, he'll have to be okay with you carrying him."

Octavia nodded and hurried out the front door.

"Is this bad? Does it mean war?" Stress rolled off Mia as she turned to face him, the robe she'd cinched around her waist loose, revealing the soft curve of her breasts.

"Truthfully, it's likely nothing. Or it will end up being nothing. But we don't take any breaches lightly in the Nova realm. There's a reason we've held strong for thousands of years."

Nodding, she wrapped her arms around herself. "Will it be easier if... I stay here? I know you can fly faster without me."

Frowning, he pulled her into his arms. "I'm not leaving you behind."

"It's okay," she said, sliding her arms around him and laying her head against his chest with a comfortableness he was getting used to.

"Do you want to stay?"

She paused, but shook her head. "Not without you." It sounded like a confession.

A very welcome one. "Then it's settled. We'll head out after we eat. You'll need to ride me or to let me carry you," he finally said.

"Pretty sure I already know how to ride you." Her tone was tart as she looked up at him.

He let out a startled burst of laughter and claimed her mouth. Goddess, this female had completely undone him. He wasn't going to be able to let her go, that much he knew. She already owned every part of him.

# CHAPTER 36

"I can't believe how fast you flew us back." There was awe in Mia's voice as Tiber shifted back to his human form in front of her home—for now.

Because soon he'd be insisting she move in with him. He wasn't certain how things worked with humans, however. He wanted her to move in right now but was worried he'd push her too fast. It went against his very nature to resist the urge to claim her, but humans were different.

He had to be mindful of that.

"I hope the flight wasn't too rough." He slid his pants on since there were others sitting outside their homes, watching him and Mia with clear interest.

"No, it was exhilarating." Laughing lightly, she patted her windblown hair, her braid mostly undone after the flight. "I almost felt like I was the one flying. I still can't believe we're here in time for a late lunch. You really did fly slowly for us on the trip up there."

Ilmari chirped as he threw himself in the grass a bit theatrically and then rolled over onto his back, his wings spread out.

As Mia shook her head at Ilmari, Angel strode out of her place, nodding politely at her. Tiber noticed he kept a decent distance between himself and Mia and his dragon preened slightly under the surface.

*That's right, Angel knows we can take him out if he gets too close to our female.*

"Your place is the same as you left it," Angel said.

"Oh, thank you. I didn't realize you'd been staying here."

"I rotated with two others, but yes, we all stayed here in case that vampire tried anything. But none of us ever saw a hint of him or anyone in his coven near your home."

"Well, thank you and the others then. You've all been so kind, and I really appreciate it."

Angel gave a brief nod. "Tiber deserves most of the thanks. He personally organized the rotation list here and the one at the castle to watch the movements of the coven."

"Thank you." She beamed up at him and her smile was like the sun coming out. For a moment he forgot to breathe.

How had he ever lived without her? All he could do was nod, then clear his throat as he looked back at Angel. "Did you see Kirkurte and Cordro?"

"Yes, I'll discuss that with you later, but Starlena left instructions for them."

He nodded, understanding that they couldn't discuss this where anyone might overhear. But at least he knew they'd made it here.

"Also, it is probably nothing, but when the coven crossed over one of the vampires came back in a state about something. Swore she'd left something and demanded the guards allow her access to her rooms."

Mia frowned as she looked between him and Angel. "What did she forget?"

"A necklace—which was found and returned to her. But I thought I would mention it."

Tiber frowned now as well. "Did the guards ever leave the portal unguarded during this time?" They had made that mistake once in the past when Princess Stella left for New Orleans and the queen had thoroughly punished the two for their oversight.

"No. They followed protocol, sent a message to the castle, then waited for one of the servants to return. The servants then escorted her back to the castle where her necklace was retrieved. She was then escorted back to the exit. Octavia left before all this to let you know about their departure and... the other thing." Angel's frown hadn't lessened.

"What?"

"The whole thing felt almost like theater. This noble vampire somehow forgot her jewelry? An expensive necklace she claims is an heirloom. I know vampires and dragons are not the same, but I find it hard to believe she accidentally left a priceless piece of jewelry. A dragon would never make that mistake. And I don't think she did either. Something of that value would have been the first thing she packed up." He lifted a shoulder. "But what do I know?"

"You think it was a ploy of some kind?" Mia said then looked at Tiber, eyebrows raised.

"I have no way of knowing, but you'll be staying with me until we figure it out." It was the perfect excuse to insist she remain at his place. Perhaps he could simply move all her things to his home a little at a time? She might not notice, and then once she couldn't live without him, she wouldn't care.

Mia blinked up at him. "Is there a question in there?"

He paused, aware of Angel watching him closely. He cleared his throat. "Either you stay with me or I stay with you."

She closed her eyes for a long moment, then surprised him with her little snort of laughter. "You are consistent, I'll give you that. Fine, we can stay at your place, but I'm bringing over more stuff this time."

Did she think that would bother him? "You can either point out everything you want, or make a list and someone will bring your things."

"You might regret that later," she said a little haughtily.

Never. She was his mate. Their fates were entwined.

# CHAPTER 37

Mia felt like a new person when she came out of the shower wrapped in her robe and her hair up in a towel. That ride on Tiber had been wild, their speed so fast she'd been more grateful than she'd expected for the goggles he'd given her.

She hadn't needed them with Ilmari but with Tiber... she wanted to ride on him again. In more ways than one.

As she headed down the hallway from the bathroom to the open living space and kitchen, one of the arched doors was open and she saw all her stuff sitting at the end of the bed.

Frowning, she stepped inside and realized that Angel or whoever had brought a lot of her things... and left them in the guest living space.

"I don't want you to feel like you have to share my space. My bedding is upstairs, but my personal room is just across the hall," Tiber said from behind her.

Painting on a pleasant expression, she gave him a small smile.

"I didn't want you to think I was expecting anything or for you to feel pressured," he added.

Pressured? After they'd just shared a day of nonstop sex. What a load of crap. "Okay."

He watched her closely for a long moment. "Okay?"

"I'll stay in here. Now if you'll excuse me, I need to get changed." She nudged him out of the bedroom and shut the door in his face, more annoyed than she could have imagined.

If Tiber wanted her, he needed to claim her. She wasn't playing games, but she remembered what he'd said the first time she'd met him. There was no way she was going to push him into publicly accepting her or for anything else for that matter. She was well aware of their class differences. In more ways than one considering she was a human.

Sure, maybe he was being polite, or whatever, but she knew enough about supernaturals that when they wanted something, especially a mate, they went for it. No holds barred.

Especially dragons.

They were obnoxious to the point that they were borderline barbarians.

The fact that Tiber wasn't pursuing her now that they were back at the castle... it hit low in her gut.

She might have tried to tell herself that she was okay with just sex between the two of them, but she'd changed her mind. She wanted more from the ancient dragon and if he wanted more from her, he'd have to make that crystal clear.

She'd spent the majority of her childhood taking care of others. Then she'd been in one shitty relationship after another and had found herself making excuses for why her relationships were always lopsided in effort.

She refused to put more into something if she wasn't receiving the same kind of effort. Even if it hurt to pull back, she had to protect her heart.

Because Tiber was the only male who'd ever had the capability to actually break it. Though who was she kidding, even now it sliced deep that he wasn't going after her the way dragons claimed their mates.

It was because she was human; she wasn't good enough.

***

Mia hadn't been expecting anyone to show up tonight, especially since she, Tiber and Ilmari had just returned a few hours ago, and it sounded like he would be heading out in the morning. But by the time she'd dried her hair and changed into comfortable clothes, the same group of warriors who'd been over the day before they'd left had brought food and a lot of cakes—and Tiber was nowhere to be seen.

"Why are there so many cakes?" she asked Octavia as she cut herself a piece.

She was almost certain the three-tiered blue and green confection was from Isaac's bakery since it had his signature style.

Octavia just laughed and winked at her. "Ha ha." Then she snagged Mia's plate right from her hand.

"Wha... hey!" But the other woman was gone, having disappeared into the next room where she threw herself down on a giant pillow and started eating her cake.

"Gotta be faster than Octavia when it comes to desserts." Nolan stepped up next to her as she started to cut another piece.

"Clearly," she grumbled before cutting another slice.

She didn't actually care about the cake, but she was annoyed that Tiber had put her in the guest room and that he was now gone without a word.

He'd left hours ago and she was in his home with all his friends and... she kind of wanted to cry. She might have joked with him about being a temperamental artist, but she wasn't.

No, she was confused and hurt and wondering what the hell was going on with them. Not that it seemed there was a "them" at this point, if the way he was acting was any indication. Since she didn't want to disappear to the guest room, she headed to the living room where they were all playing a different game than the other night.

This one involved dice and little pieces and some kind of betting that she didn't totally understand.

"Don't even think about it, cake thief." She sidestepped Octavia and sat in between Cyprus and Angel.

When Octavia opened her mouth to respond, Ilmari snuck in and licked up the last piece of the stolen cake—sending everyone into a burst of laughter.

Even Mia.

Ilmari seemed quite proud of himself, doing a little bow before he hopped into the kitchen, likely in search of more food.

She wasn't sure how much time passed, maybe another hour or two, as the others continued betting each other. As she dozed on the cushions, resting her head on Cyprus's shoulder—and debating a polite way to either ask them all to leave or to simply make her escape and get some sleep—Tiber finally stalked in looking exhausted and cranky.

His gaze narrowed on Cyprus, then her, then back to Cyprus. And he looked annoyed—with her.

She lifted her head and frowned at him, ready to ask him where he'd been when he snarled at everyone.

"Get out. Everyone but Mia—and Ilmari—out. Now."

Neptune was still with Jonothon, otherwise she was certain he'd be included too.

"Come on assholes, let's go." Octavia was on her feet first, but then she disappeared into the kitchen while everyone stood.

Smothering a yawn, she intentionally ignored Tiber and followed Octavia to find her cutting off another hunk of cake and putting it on a plate to take with her.

"I think you might have an addiction," she murmured.

"You're not wrong." Octavia snickered, but sobered when Tiber stalked into the room, a dark cloud as he continued to glower at her.

"I swear to god that glare better not be for me," Mia snapped against her better judgment. Though she took pleasure in the way his amber-gold eyes widened in surprise. "You know what... I'm stepping outside for some air. Do not follow me." And she wasn't asking for permission either.

Octavia headed out with her, eating cake as they walked past the magical barrier of his home's entrance. They were far enough away from the actual castle that the moon and a blanket of stars were their main illumination.

"What is going on with him?" Mia whispered when they were outside. Since she'd forgotten her coat, she wrapped her arms around herself to brace against the cold.

The others were trickling out and moving past them, so Octavia held a finger up to her mouth, then shooed some of the others to go faster. It was clear that Nolan was trying to wait for her, but Octavia gave him her back, tossing her dark hair over her shoulder as she did.

Mia raised her eyebrows at her, but Octavia simply shook her head.

"Okay, cake thief, talk! I'm about to lose my mind with Tiber." She was surprised he hadn't followed her out, but maybe she shouldn't be. "He put all my stuff in the guest room and told me he didn't want to pressure me even after we..." She made a gesture with her hands, making Octavia snicker.

"Oh, I know. We *all* know. I scented it at the retreat. I can *still* scent him on you. It's why we brought all the desserts and food... we were celebrating." Octavia's pretty face dipped into a frown. "But then Tiber disappeared so I thought maybe we got it wrong."

"Got what wrong?"

Octavia looked a little panicked and instead of answering, she shoved more cake in her mouth.

Beyond annoyed at this point, Mia smacked the plate out of her hand lightning fast, making it fall to the grass.

Octavia made a sad groaning sound as she stared at the fallen food. "Not the cake."

"Screw the cake. Talk."

"I thought humans were supposed to be all meek," she muttered.

"You thought that based on your vast experience with us?"

"Fair point." Then she sighed. "Look, Tiber is... he can be..." She covered her face with her hands. "I don't know what to say."

"How about the truth? I know enough about dragons and supernaturals that if they're interested in someone, they go for it and they don't care what anyone thinks. Clearly, it's a big deal that I'm a human—"

"That's not it."

"It's not?"

Looking almost guilty, Octavia shook her head. "No. I think maybe me and the others got into his head. We stopped by earlier to drop your stuff off. You were in the shower, I think. When he went to put your stuff in his room we might have told him that humans didn't like it when their partners were presumptuous about such things. That he should let you decide if you wanted to comingle your things."

"First, you have no experience with humans. Second, we're not a monolith. Third... I'm just going to talk to Tiber because this is ridiculous." If he rejected her then so be it. At least she would know. But she had to get over her own bullshit and just ask him what he wanted. And she was going to tell him what *she* wanted.

Because she wasn't going to hide her head in the sand anymore. She was going to start making better decisions when it came to relationships.

"I'm sorry, we're all crap with relationships. We know nothing. Clearly. None of us are mated."

Mated. Wait... what? She put a mental pin in that, unsure if she and Octavia were even on the same page. "No, this is on me. I should have just talked to him earlier instead of getting my feelings hurt and retreating." But that was her thing, something she needed to work on. She had to stop running.

Octavia shrugged. "I mean, you're not wrong. Dragons can be intense so it makes sense that you expected him to be more explicit in what he wanted. Especially since, you know..."

"Know what?"

Again with the panicked look. Then to Mia's horror, Octavia started taking off her clothes. "I gotta go. I hear someone calling me."

"You're such a liar." But Mia turned around as the other woman completely stripped and then with a whoosh of noise, took to the skies.

"Freaking dragons." She stalked back across the grass, determined to hash this out—and hopefully end the night in a lot of sex.

Because this wasn't solely on Tiber. It was on her too. She needed to communicate better. They both did.

She'd made it halfway across the grass to his place when she heard another whoosh and started to turn, thinking Octavia had returned (maybe to eat her fallen cake). Then froze when she felt claws wrap around her neck, pressing into her pulse point.

"Scream and I'll rip out your jugular," a terrifyingly familiar voice hissed into her ear.

# CHAPTER 38

Tired of waiting, Tiber strode outside to find Mia—with the intention of dragging her back inside and fucking her senseless.

He'd screwed up, he realized that now.

He was done pretending to be someone he wasn't. He was a dragon and she was the greatest treasure of all. So he would do what dragons did best—hoard his treasure and keep her safe.

Even if it meant kidnapping her.

But the moment he stepped into the cool night air he tasted her fear on the wind.

Without conscious thought, his beast took over, magic and energy bursting in the air as he shifted to his dragon. His camouflage fell into place as he tracked the scent up the side of the mountain.

Mia's sweet orange blossom scent mixed with something sinister—the vampire.

And the male was moving fast with her, his vampiric speed likely the same as Tiber's. Some vampires could fly. Not in the same sense that dragons could, but some of the powerful ones could make short flights with magic. Even without it, they ran at such rapid speed they might as well be flying.

Rage burned through him, driving him onward as he flew up the side of the mountain higher and higher until he crested the peak.

As he reached it, dark magic blasted him back. His beast prepared to breathe fire, but he paused, realizing the magic wasn't for him specifically.

There was a barrier of sorts in place, likely invisible to the naked eye, but in dragon form he could see a faint outline pulsing in the air, moving across the snow cap at vampiric speed.

He crested higher for a better view, trying to keep his head instead of releasing fire and blasting the entire top of the mountain.

To save Mia, he had to be the skilled warrior he was, not the wild animal that wanted to take over and simply destroy everything.

The only thing that gave him a kernel of hope was that the vampire had taken her alive. It wouldn't be for anything good, but he still wanted her alive.

Now Tiber had to get to them before the male hurt her. The vampire was a dead male walking.

Only a fool with a death wish took a dragon's mate in dragon territory.

Roughly a hundred miles later, the pulsing bubble of magic slowed, then stopped. He swooped lower, his night vision allowing him to see through the spell work.

*Mia.*

His sweet, wonderful Mia.

She was alive.

And he could once again draw in a full breath. The tension around his chest was impossibly tight, but his mate was alive.

As the vampire dumped Mia on the ground and stalked away into a cave, the magical bubble moved with him. And as it did, Tiber spotted the opening.

At his age and power level, he could simply rip through the spell with raw magic.

But it would take time and put Mia in danger.

So instead of being a battering ram, he forced his beast to shift back to human and barely slipped through one of the openings, careful not to touch the dark magic, as the bubble pulsed around the cave.

Still in camouflage, he crept on bare feet over the boulders along the top of the cave, crouching down as he peered over.

He wanted to call out to Mia, to let her know that he was there and she was safe, but he couldn't give himself away.

That was when he realized that she wasn't even bound. The fool hadn't even tied her hands, which meant he didn't view her as a threat.

The vampire really was all ego.

Tiber could hear movement inside the cave as he moved right to the edge of the drop-off. As soon as the vampire walked out, he was dead.

But as he moved, a couple smaller rocks skittered off the edge, scattering below. Fuck. He paused, and so did the sound inside.

Then to his surprise, Mia picked up a handful of pebbles and threw them at the cave opening.

"Come on, you coward! I'm not afraid of you! You're nothing but a weak baby who doesn't like being told no."

What the hell was she doing? A red haze descended over his vision as the vampire flew out of the cave, aiming right at Mia.

Letting his rage snap free, Tiber dove off the top of the cave and tackled the vampire to the ground below with a crunch of bones. He didn't even care what he'd broken, just that he'd caused the vampire pain.

It wouldn't be enough—nothing would ever be enough for this monster. And though he wanted to toy with his prey, to disembowel him, then rip him apart limb from limb while the vamp was conscious, right now wasn't about him.

He had to end this threat for Mia.

So instead of staking him to the ground and tearing off pieces of him inch by inch, he grabbed the male by the top of the head. As Charles screamed in agony, Tiber yanked back to hold him in place and punched through his back and ribs to rip out his heart.

The vampire burst into ash in a rush of wind, the fight over before it had even started. That had been no fight at all, the male not a worthy adversary. Just some pathetic entitled asshole who thought to take his Mia.

"Tiber!" Mia screamed. "Show yourself!"

He let his camouflage drop and raced at her, scooping her up as she threw herself into his arms. He hated that he was covered in blood and ash, but there was no way around it. "Goddess, why were you antagonizing him?" he breathed out, actually trembling as he held her close. He'd come so close to losing her.

"I knew that was you on top of the cave—or I assumed it was. And I thought he might have heard you, so I started throwing rocks at him to distract him."

"You have a lot of faith in me."

"I knew you would come for me," she whispered as he pulled back to look at her, to truly inspect her.

There were shallow slices around her neck, but he couldn't see any bruises. "Did he... are you okay? Physically?"

"I'm okay-ish." Her words came out raspy, but he heard the steel behind them. "He scared me more than anything. But other than grabbing me, he didn't hurt me. He was going to though." Her gaze strayed to where he used to be, now simply ash on the wind, and she shuddered. "What a fool."

His thoughts exactly. "Let's get you home. My home," he added with a growl.

She nodded, still holding onto him tightly.

"Where you will sleep in my room or up in my bed. Always."

Her eyes widened slightly, but she nodded again.

"You understand what I'm saying? You're mine, Mia. I'm obsessed and possessive and I don't even like you sitting next to other males. I'll live with it, but I'll never like it. I want you with me always, even on missions. I know it's not realistic, but I'm trying to show you who I am. I'm also fighting the urge to take you to the mountains to hide you away from everyone because you're so fucking beautiful and so fucking mine, that I don't want to share you with the world. And I know that's the mating instinct riding me hard, but I'm trying to be honest because I think it's what you need. And it's what I need. I don't want to start off our mating on a lie. I'm utterly obsessed with you."

She stared at him for a long moment, and he couldn't get a read on her scent or expression. But when she gently cupped his cheek, he turned into her hold. "No one is taking anyone to the mountains," she said quietly. "But I'm with you on the honesty. I thought I could live with just sex—" At his growl, she pressed a finger over his mouth and shushed him. "But I can't. I want everything from you, Tiber. I never expected you and I'm not giving you up... I think we need to wait on the official mating thing—"

"I might give you a week," he growled. "But no more."

She murmured something about his possessiveness before leaning up and brushing her lips over his.

Though he wanted to deepen it, to take her right then and there, he shoved back all the urges riding him. Before they did anything, he needed to get her away from her past and fly her back to her future.

# CHAPTER 39

Mia had slept like the dead last night, didn't even remember dreaming after they'd returned to Tiber's place. He'd sent Ilmari with a message to let the queen know what had happened, but Mia hadn't even cared. Charles was dead and the threat was over.

She could finally rest, safe in the knowledge that he was never going to bother her or hurt her family and friends again. There was no longer an invisible threat hanging overhead, always buzzing at the back of her mind.

Once Tiber had brought her back to his place, she'd been asleep even before he had returned to bed—his bed, though maybe she should start thinking of it as theirs? He'd been pretty insistent about that, and she didn't hate it. And she was glad that he'd been okay sleeping in the bedroom instead of up in the giant hammock. She loved it up there, but she'd needed to be a bit more grounded.

She was still reeling from everything that had happened and wanted to talk to Tiber more about... everything.

But he wasn't in his room, so she made her way to the bathroom, brushed her teeth, and tossed her clothes in his laundry hamper.

As she headed back to his room, she started going over the things she needed to do today, with the main one being that she had to pick Neptune up.

She paused as she heard a sound, then realized it was Tiber talking to Ilmari if the responsive chirps were anything to go by. Okay, adorable.

She waited for a moment as she heard them having a conversation before she called out, "Tiber, I need your help."

It didn't take him long to hurry to his room, and she loved the way he froze in the open doorway.

Naked on his bed, she spread her thighs wider for him as he stalked into the room, kicking the door shut behind him. And there was no other word because he was stalking her like she was his prey.

Prey that very much wanted to be caught.

When she reached between her legs and touched herself, he sucked in a breath, his eyes flickering to a brilliant pulsing gold as he watched her. "I was coming back here to feed you," he growled as he reached the end of the bed.

"Maybe you can eat me instead."

He groaned as the bed dipped under his weight. "Fuck, you're killing me."

She grinned at him, feeling like a new person after everything that had happened. She'd probably be dealing with some of the trauma later, but she wanted to enjoy this moment for what it was, wanted to enjoy everything that Tiber was.

A big, sometimes grumpy, wonderful dragon she'd never expected.

He crawled up the length of her body, just staring down at her for a long moment, the weight of everything seeming to hang between them. "I'm not good with words... but I love you."

She sucked in a breath at his admission. She understood that mating was a different beast for supernaturals and didn't always equate to love, at least not at first. "You don't have to say that simply because I'm human." Even if she loved that he had.

Using one hand to hold himself up, he slid his other between her legs, cupped her mound gently. "I know." The words a soft growl as he slid a finger along her slick folds. "I don't say things I don't mean. Not to you."

He was killing her in the best way possible. "I love you too," she managed to rasp out, glad she could still talk. And it was the truth. She'd realized it right before she'd been kidnapped, when she'd wanted to hash everything out with him instead of running. Because she loved this big male enough to want to stay and fight for him. "Even if it feels too soon," she whispered, some deep part of her wondering if they really were rushing into things.

"Says who?" He slipped a finger inside her as he leaned down, brushed his lips over hers. "We make the rules for our relationship."

She tightened around his finger, wanting a whole lot more than just that. Nipping his bottom lip, she slid her hands over his chest, stroking all that power vibrating under her fingertips. She wondered if she'd ever get used to being with him. "I'm going with you when you leave." She kept her voice pitched low as she slid her hand down his abdomen, searching out his hard length.

"We'll talk about it later." His voice was strained as she wrapped her fingers around his erection, stroked once.

"Nothing to talk about." She pushed gently at his chest with her other hand, deciding she wanted to be on top and in control. Though the control thing was probably an illusion, she still wanted to ride him.

Even though he grumbled, he rolled onto his back and let her straddle him. "I beg to differ," he growled, reaching between her legs again.

Not that she needed it, she was already wet and ready for him. The pleasure of having him teasing her overtook her brain for a moment. She'd been saying something... Oh right. "Just get used to the idea and deal with it," she managed to rasp out.

"Goddess," he gritted out as she tightened around his fingers.

She laughed, then groaned as he cupped one of her breasts, pinched, rolled her nipple in a way she'd come to enjoy.

Fuck, she needed him inside her and no more talking. She lifted up slightly and positioned herself above his thick erection before slowly sliding down his shaft. She gasped as he filled her, once again wondered if she'd ever get used to the feel and size of him.

Slowly, she began rolling her hips against his, feeling that normally elusive pleasure already starting to build each time the head of his cock hit that sweet spot deep inside her.

He held onto her hips, forcing her to slow down. "Goddess, Mia. I want to live inside you."

She was beyond words as she picked up the pace, glad when he loosened his grip, meeting her stroke for stroke in a rhythm she'd quickly become obsessed with.

Because he wasn't the only one obsessed; she never wanted to be apart from him. Maybe that would fade with time, but right now she couldn't even imagine it as he brought her the most exquisite pleasure.

She wasn't sure how much time passed, but he eventually took over, because of course he did, and she found herself bent over in front of him as he wrapped his fingers around her throat. He held her so gently yet so possessively as he thrust into her from behind, the growls he made as he nipped at her neck primal and everything she'd always wanted.

Everything about being with him was raw and earthy and she loved that there were no barriers between them. Just pleasure.

She didn't even have to tell him that she was close, he clearly sensed it because he dropped his hand down to her clit and began stroking in tune with his thrusts—sending her over the edge.

Stars burst in front of her eyes as her climax punched through her. He held onto one of her hips as he rode the wave with her, coming inside her in hard thrusts as they both lost themselves in each other.

Eventually they collapsed onto his sheets, but instead of letting her lie there, he turned her over and tugged her onto his chest.

"We're mating as soon as I get back," he growled into the quiet room.

"That doesn't sound like a question." She was still drowsy with pleasure as she traced a finger over one of his pecs.

"Good, because I'm not asking."

"Is it messed up that I like how bossy you are?"

He lazily played with one of her breasts, making her gasp.

"But I'm still going with you," she managed to get out, because no way was he leaving without her.

He gently pinched her nipple, making her arch into his touch.

She raised her head so she could look at him. "Stop trying to distract me with pleasure."

"After everything you've been through—"

"Exactly. After everything, I don't want to be separated. And I'm not asking. I'm telling you. I'm *going*." She jutted her chin out mutinously. "You already said I wouldn't be in the way or in danger if I stayed back at your basecamp. There's no danger."

She could see that he wanted to argue, that he wanted to keep her wrapped up here in a bubble of safety. But neither of them could live like that. It would eventually destroy them, something she understood on her most primal level. And she was pretty sure he did too, because he closed his eyes and groaned.

"You have to stay at camp. No following me."

"I would never. Besides, I can't fly, how am I going to follow you?"

He grumbled as she laid her head on his chest, continued tracing along the hard lines and striations of his body.

"You'll be happy that I'm there," she added.

"Of course, I will be. I'm worried I'll never leave our tent. Or I'll put you in danger inadvertently. Or a million other things that might go wrong."

At the real note of worry in his voice, she lifted her head again. "I won't go if it bothers you that much. It's okay."

Holding her close to him, he settled one big hand on her hip, squeezed. "No. I want to agree and leave you here, but... no. You're coming. I know you'll be safe with me. Last night scared me in a way I've never experienced. I've... always been aware of my own power, but if anything were to happen to you..." Trailing off, he slid his hands through her hair, cupping the back of her neck as she leaned up to kiss him.

There was more they needed to talk about, because this fear of his was real, was emanating off him in waves she could almost feel. She would always worry for him, but he was powerful in a way she would never be physically. If anything, his enemies would be wise to give him a wide berth.

Right now, she didn't want to worry about enemies or any darkness. No, she wanted to bask in this new relationship, simply enjoy what they were starting.

# CHapter 40

*Three days later*

Mia wasn't sure what to bring for this upcoming scouting mission that Tiber had finally relented and agreed to let her go on. He'd waffled a bit, but in the end, he wanted her with him.

And she could paint anywhere. Since she'd be basically stuck at whatever basecamp he set up with the small group of warriors that were following after the others who'd gone ahead, she didn't want to get bored.

He'd told her that she could bring as much as she wanted, but she still had to be mindful about how much he could carry. Which... was probably a lot.

As she folded up another thick, wool tunic she paused at a sound downstairs. Jonothon had said he might stop by to help her.

"Jonothon?" she called out, stepping from her bedroom into the hallway. Though soon, this wouldn't be her place anymore because she was moving in with Tiber officially. She'd miss this cozy cottage that had become her home for a while, but Neptune had made it clear Tiber's place (and Ilmari's presence) were far superior so at least her cat was happy.

When no response was forthcoming, dread settled low in her abdomen. Likely an overreaction, but after being threatened for months, then kidnapped by her ex a few days ago, she was allowed some paranoia.

Moving quickly, and only feeling a little paranoid, she unzipped the small cache of poisons Tiber had given her, then dipped the small blade he'd also given her into two of them because she couldn't remember which was which. Pink would paralyze and eventually kill and the green one... maybe kill? Craaaap, what did they do?

Feeling only a little foolish, she moved quietly to the window and looked outside to see if anything was out of the ordinary. It was midday so she wasn't surprised to see the grassy area between all their residences empty. Everyone was likely working or in some cases, napping.

In about an hour people would start trickling outside to take breaks or eat, but until then... She moved away from the window, keeping the blade clutched down by her side as she weighed her options.

Someone was here.

Not Jonothon, or he'd have answered her.

Heart in her throat, she eased open the bedroom window even though it was freezing, and pushed the curtains outside. They flapped with the breeze, and she hoped that made it look like she'd climbed down from the second floor.

Which she would do if she could, but it was too high up. She'd break something if she tried to jump and then she'd be sitting prey with broken bones.

Trying to keep her breathing steady even though her pulse was racing, she moved to the other side of her room and heard a squeak on the stairs.

She ducked behind her open doorway as a shadow flitted past her door.

Clutching the handle of the blade tightly, she waited as the intruder stepped further into her bedroom. The footsteps were quiet enough, but she could sense the movement and took a chance to peek around the door.

A tall, hooded figure was standing by the window, peering outside.

Mia could either stay behind the door and hope she wasn't discovered or try to sneak out of here.

When the hooded figure leaned out a bit more as if they were going to climb out, she decided to just go for it and eased out from behind the door without touching it.

She stepped silently through the doorway and into the hallway but must have made a sound because the figure suddenly turned.

All she could see was the glowing red eyes of menace before she sprinted down the hallway, screaming as she ran. With the window open, she could only hope someone nearby might hear her.

Otherwise, she was on her own.

As she reached the end of the hallway, the intruder barreled into her like a football player, sending her flying toward the top of the stairs with a scream of her own.

Her attacker was a woman.

Mia cried out in pain as she slammed against the stone wall, then slumped onto the landing with a thud, her bones bruised from the impact. Everything was hazy in front of her as she blinked, tried to regain her senses.

Fingers with sharp nails wrapped around her neck, wrenched her to her feet.

Mia struggled, trying to pry the claws from around her neck. The tall female's hood slipped off her head, revealing the blonde who'd always been friendly with her.

Fjola!

Pain pierced Mia's throat as she struggled to hold onto her blade.

"You killed the male I love," Fjola snarled. "He would have come back to me, he always did! But you ruined it."

Mia clawed at the woman's hand, trying to kick out at her, but Fjola just laughed as she squeezed harder.

Shoving out with her other arm, Mia swiped at the vampire, slicing through the woman's hood and tunic, making contact with her skin as she tried to impale her somewhere. *Anywhere.* If she could even just slow her down and get away.

Fjola looked down suddenly, laughed maniacally as she batted the blade out of Mia's hand. It clattered to the floor with a finality she felt to her bones.

This was it. She was going to die.

"You can't do anything right! I have no idea what he ever saw in you. And if I hadn't helped him sneak back in with that vanishing spell..." She blinked suddenly and the grip on Mia started to loosen as the blonde stared at her, open-mouthed, her eyes now amber instead of the maniacal red.

Mia kicked at the woman again and this time, Fjola let go completely as she crumpled onto the landing with a groan.

Sucking in bucketfuls of air, Mia hurriedly crawled over her, trying to get to the stairs. As she managed to make it over the prone woman, she felt her strength returning with each clear breath.

Behind her, Fjola gasped wildly, clutching at her throat as she rolled onto her back. Her skin had gone a pale gray as she seemed to disintegrate in front of Mia.

She must have nicked her with the poisoned blade.

Forcing herself to move, Mia picked up the fallen blade but couldn't stop staring as the female continued crumbling into nothing but ashes.

As she finally pushed up to her feet, her front door burst open.

She raced down the rest of the stairs to find Tiber racing in, eyes wide.

"She's dead," Mia managed to rasp out through her bruised throat as she dropped the blade. She didn't need it anymore. "Poison."

He moved faster than she could track, scooping her up and carrying her out of the house with a gentleness she hadn't expected.

Later she would ask him how he'd known or why he was there, but for now, it was over. Or she really hoped it was.

And she'd saved herself this time.

# CHapTer 41

*One month later*

Mia wasn't sure how long Tiber had been in their shared tent—which was a lot different than she'd originally envisioned. She'd been expecting something small and basic from her Girl Scout days.

Not this luxury "tent" the size of her first apartment, and held up with some kind of aluminum rods. Tiber and his crew all had large tents like theirs as well as furniture and lots and lots of pillows and blankets. Glamping on steroids. Because, apparently, dragons here liked comfortable things. This was the kind of camping she could get on board with.

She'd set up her canvas and supplies on the west side of their accommodations a few hours ago and realized how long she'd been working when she felt the stiffness in her back. She stood from her seat when she saw Tiber in the entryway on the opposite side, just watching her.

Her heart skipped a beat at the sight of him. Wearing only loose pants and no shirt, he was an artist's dream. Her dream. "Hey, how long have you been here?"

"Not long." His voice was a deep rumble as he stepped further into the space. "I like watching you work and didn't want to disturb you."

She set her brush in the nearby container of water and made her way to the seating area and him.

He came over to pull her into his lap and nuzzled her neck as he held her close with an exhausted sigh. "Negotiations went well today," he finally murmured. "I think we'll be able to return home soon."

She ran a soothing hand over his back, wanting to comfort him. She knew that he had to be exhausted by now and wished there was more that she could do for him. "That's good." She didn't know everything about the mission he and the others were on. Just that his particular guard was camped out on top of a small, but heavily wooded mountain. The forest gave them protection from any aerial spies and was about a hundred miles away from where intruders had set up their own camp right on the edge of one of the portals to the Nova realm.

No one particularly wanted bloodshed (okay, some of the dragons definitely did), but they were at the point where either the interlopers gave in and left, or they were dead.

She wasn't sure of all the particulars, but it was serious enough that Starlena was there and had been negotiating with their leader for weeks before Tiber's guard even arrived. The interlopers thought they were owed something that had to do with a feud from millennia ago and... Mia hadn't retained most of it.

She just knew that Tiber was on alert the majority of the day, along with his people and she wanted him safe. Tiber and his people stuck to the shadows making sure none of the interlopers got out of line or tried to move farther into the realm. More than anything, he'd seemed bored by this particular mission, said the only bright spot of his days was when he got to return to her.

And even though she could lose herself in her work, she'd missed him as well. He was the bright spot in her day and at times she'd found herself just counting down until he returned.

"I think we have a few hours until the evening meal. Feel like entertaining ourselves for a while?" She nipped his earlobe, enjoying the way his entire body rumbled in agreement underneath her. She couldn't do a lot for him, but she would give him pleasure—and take some for herself. Because he was the most giving lover she'd ever had. "I'll take that as a yes."

"Let me close the flaps first." He nipped her back and started to slide her off him when Ilmari flew through one of the openings and tumbled face-first onto a cluster of the oversized pillows.

Quickly following him was Octavia, her expression... weird. "So, you've got some guests." She was giving Tiber a strange look, her eyes unnaturally wide.

"Is it the invaders?" he growled, sliding Mia off him completely as he stood, looking ready to rip someone's head off.

Part of Mia loved it when he went all "Tiber" on anyone. She wasn't sure what that said about her, but she loved all sides of him, especially his intense ones.

"I wish."

Ilmari had finally managed to untangle himself and started hopping around manically next to Octavia, chirping away until she finally hushed him.

Ilmari blew a raspberry at the warrior, who just gave him an exasperated "shush" before looking back at the two of them. "Your parents are here, Tiber."

"Wait... what?" Tiber looked confused and lost in a way she'd never expected from the big dragon. "You must be mistaken."

Moments later two tall, large individuals strode past Octavia and a now very quiet Ilmari, into the tent.

"Nope," Octavia whispered before she practically ran to one of the nearby tents.

Ilmari hovered in the entrance, staring up at the two dragon shifters in human form, then let out a little squeak before hopping after Octavia.

Mia stood next to Tiber, sliding her hand into his as the two barely dressed warriors strode into the tent, smiling broadly at their son.

They both had dark hair, though his mother's had streaks of pale blonde in hers. Their skin was a dark bronze, with almost an undertone of the same amber-gold of Tiber's eyes and scales. They wore no shoes and had matching tattoos; hers along her right arm, his along his left. When they stood next to each other it was so clear that they were a unit. A mated couple.

"Well? Aren't you going to welcome us?" his mother demanded.

Tiber cleared his throat, her words seeming to pull him out of his head as he stepped forward. "Mother, Father, please, welcome. I'm just stunned you're here, that's all. How did you even—"

"Starlena allowed us passage, of course."

"Ah." After greeting his parents with that arm clasp so many warriors used, they also hugged him one at a time with a fierceness that made it clear how much they loved their son.

Mia couldn't help but have a moment of panic wondering what they would think of her. She was nothing like the dragon females of his guard or even most of the ones she knew at the castle.

"Mia, these are my parents, Rhiannon and Rakeshar."

To her surprise, they both hugged her, though thankfully more gently than the way they'd hugged Tiber.

"What a pleasure to meet you, Mia." His mother took both her hands as she stepped back. "We heard about Tiber's mating and couldn't wait to meet you. And you are lovelier than I even imagined."

She didn't seem disappointed, which soothed any lingering doubt she'd had about what his family would think about her being a human. "Thank you. It's a pleasure to meet you as well. Would you like tea or... I think we have some snacks around here."

"Sit," Tiber murmured, kissing the top of her head. "I'll get everything."

Oh, no. She wanted to insist that she get everything, but it was clear he needed a moment.

"Hot tea would be wonderful," his father boomed. "We've been flying for an age. So Starlena tells us that you'll be heading home soon."

"Ah, yes," Tiber said as he set the copper pot on the interior stove they'd been using to cook smaller meals and heat their tea. "That's the hope anyway. This has been the most tedious of trips and we're all ready to be done with this place."

Mia had enjoyed all her nights with Tiber but knew how exhausted he was and wanted to return home more for his sake than hers.

"Hopefully you've been making time for your new mate, son." His father hadn't sat yet, was pacing around the space and stopped in front of her only finished canvas.

It was a silly painting of Ilmari hanging upside down from one of the trees, wings spread wide, a sense of wonder on his sweet face. He seemed to love posing for her and he was probably the best model she'd ever had. The dragonling could remain in one pose for hours if needed.

She'd added sprites flying around him for whimsy and Ilmari had given it his "chirp of approval" once she'd finally finished.

"Of course, I have," Tiber said, his voice tight.

"You're very talented, Mia," his father continued, seeming oblivious to Tiber's tone.

"Why are you two here? Is something wrong?" Tiber said before Mia could respond.

Mia whipped her gaze to him, surprised at his hard tone. "Tiber."

"Oh no, dear, it's a fair question. We haven't been to see him in... ages." His mother patted Mia's arm gently as she looked at her son.

"But we heard humans are very fertile, so we wanted to be the first to congratulate you on your mating," his father said.

"Yes," his mother said, nodding along. "And we would like to discuss names of your future children. I've heard that humans can have multiple births at a time."

Mia's mouth dropped open as her gaze ping-ponged between the two of them. She was glad she hadn't been drinking tea because she might have spit it out.

"We are not having children anytime soon." Tiber looked at Mia for confirmation.

All she could do was nod. They'd officially mated the first night they'd arrived here, so now they were linked on a deeper level, and she wasn't quite human, but also not immortal in the sense that Tiber was. But she was stronger and harder to kill than before, something that pleased both of them. Children weren't on their radar right now. Not even close.

She cleared her throat, stunned by this conversation as much as their appearance. "We've only just mated, and I would like to enjoy my new mate for some time."

"Of course, of course." His mother patted her hand again. "I remember what it was like when we first mated. We holed up in a cave for... oh, six months or so." She looked at her mate adoringly, and then at Tiber as he handed her a cup of tea. "We just missed you. That's the real reason we're here."

"I've missed you as well. And I'm glad you're here to meet my mate." After giving his father tea, he sat on the cushions next to Mia, sliding her onto his lap without pause.

Loving how affectionate he was, she curled against him as the four of them talked for the next couple hours. And despite what his mother had said about simply missing him, it was clear that they thought humans popped out babies like cats because of all the questions they had.

Even though they offered to let his parents stay with them, they opted to sleep out in the open air in their dragon form higher up on the mountain.

When darkness had fallen and it was just the two of them in the quiet tent once again, Tiber buried his face against her head with a groan. "I swear I've never met those two weirdos in my life. I have no idea what's gotten into them. Those are not the dragons who raised me."

She snickered even as she melted into his arms. "They probably just miss you."

"Maybe," he murmured, raking his teeth along her neck. "But right now and for the rest of the night, I don't want to think about or talk about them at all."

"Me neither," she whispered right before he claimed her mouth.

Not long after that, he claimed her again and again—and she claimed him right back.

She might not have expected this dragon, but she would be forever grateful to the goddess or whatever higher power there was, for putting him in her path.

She had a feeling they were going to butt heads more than once—he had the strongest personality of anyone she'd ever met. He liked to give orders and expected everyone to follow.

And while she loved that in the bedroom, she was certain they'd have some tests in their future. But she had no doubt they were meant for each other, because obsession didn't even begin to cover how she felt about him. She loved the dragon and had no doubt how much he loved her. It was clear in every little thing he did.

And she was never letting him go.

# CHAPTER 42

*Dear Robin,*

*Things have been wild around the castle but I'm counting down until you get here! Tiber's parents just left after staying with us for a couple months. They're wonderful, though Tiber swears that they've lost their minds over future grandchildren who don't exist yet and won't for a long time to come. While I've enjoyed having them, I'm thrilled to have our place to ourselves again.*

*I think Neptune and Ilmari are ready too. Oh, did I tell you that Ilmari officially lives with us now? He and Neptune are inseparable anyway so it's not like we had a choice.*

*Also, I officially heard from Charles's coven leader that there is no bad blood over his death and things are "good" between us so to speak. In reality, I think they were too scared of going head-to-head with a dragon realm, but I don't even care what the reason is. Apparently, he and Fjola had engaged in a toxic, on-again, off-again relationship for a hundred or so years. Each*

*of them would throw various relationships or significant others in the others'*
*face (something I never knew, because, of course, he didn't tell me she was an*
*ex). Regardless, I'm happy to put that chapter behind me and start fresh with*
*my new mate.*

*I can't believe I ever thought he was a jerk. You're probably sick of me writing*
*about him, but too bad. Once you get here, you'll see how wonderful he is.*
*And fair warning, you'll probably get hit on by dragons—some of them are*
*so fascinated by humans. I know you'll hold your own. Love and miss you!*

*Xo,*
*Mia*

# Dear Readers

Thank you for reading the latest book in the Ancients Rising series! Originally this was supposed to be a novella, but these characters surprised me and demanded a novel. I'm really glad they did! Since I receive this question often enough, yes, I'm planning more books in the series. I absolutely love this world so be on the lookout for more dragons in the future. If you'd like to stay in touch and be the first to learn about new releases in this series (or any book news), I post updates on social media. You can also:

Check out my website for book news: https://www.katiereus.com

Also, please consider leaving a review at one of your favorite online retailers. It's a great way to help other readers discover new books and I appreciate all reviews.

Happy reading,
Katie

# ACKnOWLeDGments

I owe a big thanks to my critique partner and bestie Kaylea Cross, who kept asking me when my main characters were finally going to kiss! I hope the wait was worth it. To Christian, thank you for another gorgeous cover. I'm also grateful to Joan for edits and to Sarah and Tammy for proofreading. Thank you as well to my ARC readers, some of whom have been reading this series since the very beginning. For my readers, y'all are the best! Thank you for all the emails and social media messages asking for more dragons. It's such a joy to release a new book into the world and hear from you. And to my two writer pups, Jack and Piper, thank you for keeping me company, the silly antics, and making sure I get outside for walks at least four times a day. Because of you, I'm not living that vampire life.

# ABOUT THE AUTHOR

**Katie Reus** is the *USA Today* bestselling author of the Ancients Rising series, the Endgame trilogy and the Redemption Harbor Series. She fell in love with reading at a young age thanks to weekly trips to the library. However, she didn't always know she wanted to be a writer. After changing majors too many times, she finally graduated with a degree in psychology. Not long after that she discovered a new love—writing.

She now spends her days writing paranormal romance and romantic suspense. In addition to writing, she's also obsessed with her dogs, hiking, quilting, and all things aviation.

# COMPLETE BOOKLIST

Saved by Darkness
Guardian of Darkness
Sentinel of Darkness
A Very Dragon Christmas
Darkness Rising

***Deadly Ops Series***
Targeted
Bound to Danger
Chasing Danger
Shattered Duty
Edge of Danger
A Covert Affair

***Endgame Trilogy***
Bishop's Knight
Bishop's Queen
Bishop's Endgame

***Holiday With a Hitman Series***
How the Hitman Stole Christmas
A Very Merry Hitman
All I Want for Christmas is a Hitman

***MacArthur Family Series***
Falling for Irish
Unintended Target
Saving Sienna

### Moon Shifter Series
Alpha Instinct

Lover's Instinct

Primal Possession

Mating Instinct

His Untamed Desire

Avenger's Heat

Hunter Reborn

Protective Instinct

Dark Protector

A Mate for Christmas

### O'Connor Family Series
Merry Christmas, Baby

Tease Me, Baby

It's Me Again, Baby

Mistletoe Me, Baby

### Red Stone Security Series®
No One to Trust

Danger Next Door

Fatal Deception

Miami, Mistletoe & Murder

His to Protect

Breaking Her Rules

Protecting His Witness

Sinful Seduction

Under His Protection

Deadly Fallout

Sworn to Protect

Secret Obsession

Love Thy Enemy

Dangerous Protector

Lethal Game

Secret Enemy

Saving Danger

Guarding Her

Deadly Protector

Danger Rising

Protecting Rebel


*Redemption Harbor® Series*

Resurrection

Savage Rising

Dangerous Witness

Innocent Target

Hunting Danger

Covert Games

Chasing Vengeance


*Redemption Harbor® Security*

Fighting for Hailey

Fighting for Reese

Fighting for Adalyn

Fighting for Magnolia

Fighting for Berlin

Fighting for Mari

Fighting for Hope

### *Sin City Series (the Serafina)*
First Surrender

Sensual Surrender

Sweetest Surrender

Dangerous Surrender

Deadly Surrender


### *Verona Bay Series*
Dark Memento

Deadly Past

Silent Protector


### *Linked books*
Retribution

Tempting Danger


### *Non-series Romantic Suspense*
Running From the Past

Dangerous Secrets

Killer Secrets

Deadly Obsession

Danger in Paradise

His Secret Past

The Trouble with Rylee

Falling for Nola

Tempted by Her Neighbor

Falling for Valentine

*Paranormal Romance*

Destined Mate

Protector's Mate

A Jaguar's Kiss

Tempting the Jaguar

Enemy Mine

Heart of the Jaguar

Made in United States
Cleveland, OH
17 August 2025

19491565R00146